BEDDING THE ENEMY

LAQUETTE

Cover Artist
TARIA A. REED
Editor
GAYLA LEATH

BEDDING THE ENEMY

LAQUETTE

To every Asian man who's never gotten to be the sexy, bad boy hero, or never gotten the girl at the end of the movie, this is for you.

ACKNOWLEDGMENTS

To God, from whom all blessings flow, thank you for the gift, the desire, the support, and the opportunity. To Damon, this does not happen without you. Love you forever. To Sterling and Semaj, my heartbeats, the best parts of me. To my family and friends, thank you for putting up with my craziness. To Gayla, thank you for making my crazy sound amazing. To Lexie Craig, thank you for supplying me with my new motto, "Hustle until you don't have to introduce yourself" (unknown). To all my JMC and LIJ people, your love strengthens me. To my Loungers, you guys hold me down and keep me going. Thank you so much for the loyalty and encouragement. To the readers, you will never know how much I appreciate your support. Thank you for taking this journey with me.

Keep it sexy,
 LaQuette 💋

BEDDING THE ENEMY

Masaki Yamaguchi has lived by one rule: Bend the world to your will, and break those that refuse to comply. This motto has served him well as the head of the Yakuza family in Canarsie, Brooklyn. However, when he meets a soulful beauty with locs from Brownsville with her own set of rules, things aren't as clear, or easy as they used to be.

Oshun Sampson has worked hard to clean up her beloved Brownsville, Brooklyn. She's sacrificed everything, including her own happiness, for the cause. She'll be damned if she allows anyone the chance to destroy the progress she and her community have made. With the looming threat of the Canarsie Yakuza family closing in, the sexy new patron with the captivating eyes is a dangerous distraction she can't afford.

Two powerful leaders with one distinct line drawn between them. Will their passion be enough to hold them together? Or, will bedding the enemy result in a bloody war that tears them and their communities apart?

1

"Yesssss Masssss," Oshun Sampson moaned, as the man above her slid his cock inside her just the right way. Her pussy walls contracted, trying their best to strangle the length of him, keeping him planted inside her, rubbing so deliciously over her G-spot.

She couldn't remember how many times he'd made her cream all over him since they'd started this round. All she knew was she could feel her next orgasm clawing at her again. Her pussy lips so slick and swollen, each stroke making them sizzle with electricity.

"Let me watch you touch yourself while I fuck you," he whispered against her lips, as he bent down to steal a kiss.

She couldn't see him behind her closed lids. She'd given up trying to keep them open; her mind so blitzed-out from the way he was stroking her. But she knew his cocky ass had that crooked smile he always wore when he knew he had her at his mercy. It was a given anytime he had his dick inside her, or had her calling on the gods and goddesses as she came, that she was in fact at his mercy.

She fought the impulse to give in to him. It wasn't in her

nature to submit to someone else's will. Oshun wasn't the kind of woman to let anyone control her. Control was always hers to wield. But, a one-night stand with a club hook-up three months ago changed all that. Now, instead of hitting it and quitting it the way she'd intended, she was laying in his bed, legs spread, pussy dripping, and hungry for his cock.

He slowed down his strokes as he bent down to kiss her again. "I know you heard me. Play with my pretty pussy and I'll let you come all over this dick again."

Her walls contracted at his promise, and a shudder spread throughout her body. As defiant as she wanted to be, she was too close and too hot not to acquiesce. She used her fingers to stroke herself slowly. Her clit was so sensitive it bordered on painful. She knew if she added too much pressure or speed, she'd tumble over into bliss.

She knew it would feel so good. But, she held back because it turned him on to watch her stroke herself. She ran her fingers from clit to slit. Her fingertips scraped against his cock every time he pushed in and pulled out. When she heard him hissing between his teeth, she knew his senses were overloaded as well.

"Faster," he commanded. "Don't fucking stop."

She sped up her motions. She could feel the familiar tension building up inside her, could feel the burning heat that seared her from the inside out. When the muscles in her thighs began twitching, and her pussy began contracting in powerful spasms, Oshun knew it wouldn't be long. Two more circular strokes and she felt herself break apart, felt her breath catch in her chest, and release spread like warm butter through her nerves.

The orgasm wrecked her, breaking her into unrecognizable pieces. Instead of helping her, Masaki Yamaguchi perpetuated her demise by slamming his cock over and over into her. It was hard and so rough, and she loved every minute of it. So much so, she begged him not to stop, begged him to keep destroying her.

He didn't disappoint. He kept hammering at her, prolonging the orgasm that ravaged her as she convulsed beneath him.

"God, you squeeze me so fucking tight, Oshun," he howled as his rhythm faltered. She felt his cock swell, and seconds later he pulsed his release into the latex barrier between them.

When he pulled out, she was still quivering, her body shaking of its own accord. Masaki must have seen her shaking as an invitation, because he rearranged himself so that his mouth met her pussy lips. His tongue gently bathed her, soothing and exciting at the same time. She'd thought he'd broken her, but within seconds, his tongue had her tensing in another release. This was sweet and gentle, but still, there he went again making her lose control.

He licked her cunt again, swirling it at her opening, groaning in satisfaction against her slick lips. He touched her once again with his tongue, finally relenting his hold over her when he heard her hiss.

Taking advantage of the reprieve she'd been given, she took a deep breath and opened her eyes. Dark eyes shining with mischief and a self-assured grin met hers. He took a moment to slowly pass that dangerous tongue of his over his lips, closing his eyes while a deep moan rumbled in his chest.

"God my pussy is so sweet."

As much as she wanted to disabuse him of the notion of him owning her sex, she knew she'd be lying. The way he kept her begging for his attention when they came together, there was no doubt in either of their minds that his fucking name was stamped across it in bright red letters.

Mas.

In every way that mattered, she certainly was. She didn't lie to herself about what and how deeply she felt for Masaki. What she felt wasn't the problem, how she lived was.

Being his was a notion she could only entertain while inside the confines of either of their homes. Here in his bed, or just a few minutes to the east in hers, she could wallow in the decadence of this man's affection, in the reckless abandon of her heart's greatest desire. But outside either of those situations, in front of the world, she could never take what she so desperately wanted; her place at his side as his woman.

He crawled up her body, pressing his mouth against hers, demanding that she open herself to him again. She barely parted her lips before his tongue was inside, painting her lips and tongue with the taste of her essence.

It was a heady experience, one that had her threading her hands through the ink-colored strands on his head, pulling him deeper into the kiss. If she weren't so fucked-out, this kiss could very well have been the start of another round for them.

She gentled the kiss, smoothing her hands carefully down his back until she met the meaty curve of his ass. She gave it a satisfying smack that pulled a wide grin from each of them.

"That never gets old," she said.

"What? You smacking my ass?"

Oshun chuckled. "That too. But I was referring to the way you fuck me until I'm boneless."

He placed a playful peck on the tip of her nose, and rolled over to the side, pulling her into the little spoon position. Dropping another peck on her shoulder, he snuggled in close behind her.

"I know a way to top me fucking you boneless," he offered.

"Not possible. No way you could improve upon perfection."

"Wanna bet?"

He rolled away from her, leaning toward the nightstand closest to him. When he reclaimed his position next to her, he handed her a square velvet box. The kind of velvet box that usually housed expensive jewelry. The thought of what could be inside this box had cold fear spilling inside her. It was only the lifetime of keeping her emotions buried from the rest of the world that allowed her to school her features.

Suppressing the shudder that threatened to spread through her, Oshun turned to Masaki, hoping the look of expectancy he wore didn't mean what she feared.

"What is this?"

"I believe in English, the word you're looking for is...gift. Typically, you have to open it to see what's inside."

Oshun sighed deeply and rolled her eyes.

"You know you're an asshole, right?"

He shrugged his shoulders and smiled. "I know you have a pretty little asshole that I plan on burying myself in once we've both recovered from our last round." He pointed to the still unopened box in her hand. "Stop stalling. Open it."

She felt the puckered skin of her rosebud contract at his words, and a slight pulse of electricity zipped through her clit. It didn't matter how he wanted to have sex with her, her body was always excited by his propositions.

Stay focused, Oshun. This isn't the time.

She opened the box, afraid of what it held, and was slightly relieved when she saw two keys resting on the cushioned bed instead of an engagement ring.

"I'm confused," she said with a shaky smile on her face. "What are these for?"

"They open my front door. This is my corny way of asking you to move in with me."

"Mas." The seriousness of her tone drained the light and easy atmosphere their lovemaking had created. She watched him tense up, pulling himself to a sitting position against the headboard.

"What, Oshun? You can save the "It's too soon" crap you're about to spew at me. We've spent nearly every day together over the last three months. You spend three to four nights a week sleeping in my bed, and the rest of the week I'm in yours. We already live together. All I'm asking is to make it official. So, if you're going to say no, at least don't insult my intelligence with a lie."

And there it was again, the one topic that always seemed to shake whatever peace they found in each other's presence. Oshun closed her eyes and pinched the bridge of her nose in frustration. It was fast becoming her conditioned response whenever Masaki brought up the topic of commitment.

"Mas, us spending nights together is totally different than us moving in together. I can't do that."

"You trying to tell me you're not there, you're not ready?"

She shook her head. Emotionally she was more than ready to make that commitment to him. Unfortunately, logic kept reminding her why it couldn't be. Her life wouldn't allow for the type of connection Mas seemed to be pushing toward more and more.

"Mas, you're so special to me. You know that. But, I've told you from the beginning I wasn't looking for a relationship. My life doesn't allow for it."

"What the fuck does that even mean, Oshun?"

He quickly swung his legs over the side of the bed, stalking to the dresser and rummaging for a pair of underwear inside. He stepped into a pair of black boxer briefs, and turned to her with his arms crossed against his chest. Standing there in the middle of the room, his full six-feet height seemed more ominous than usual.

The sharp slant of his eyes became more pronounced as his heavy gaze focused on her. His broad chest rose and fell in fast movements, his full-sleeve tattooed arms flexed with power, revealing carved, lean muscles. In that moment, she could see who he was so clearly. Japanese, strong, powerful, confident, and sexy as all fucking hell.

"You're a waitress at a club, Oshun. Single, with no kids, or dependents that I know of. I mean, that's about the simplest life I can imagine. What the hell is really holding you back?"

She cringed at the harshness in his voice. She'd led him to believe her life was simple. He could never know otherwise. Keeping that in mind, she didn't hold the insult he'd just hurled at her against him. She knew it came from a place of frustration. He was frustrated she kept pulling away from him. But more importantly, he was frustrated about not being able to understand her reasoning.

She shifted in the bed, pulling herself up against the headboard, and covered her exposed body with the sheet. When they were naked, Masaki controlled the scene. That was a fact she'd accepted with much difficulty. Gearing up to have what could prove to be their biggest argument to date, she needed to maintain what little power she could.

"It's like you said, "that you know of." You don't know me, Masaki. And the truth is, I can't really afford to let you know me. I told you that night in the club I wasn't looking for forever. I wanted to have some fun, and that was all."

He ran his fingers angrily through the tapered dark waves on his head, then dropped his hands to the cut vee of his hips.

"Are you fucking someone else? Is that what this is about, keeping your options open?"

She shook her head, looking up toward the ceiling hoping for strength. Strength to keep her temper in check, strength to keep her emotions corralled, and strength to not give in to what they both wanted.

She pulled the covers off, and planted her feet firmly on the ground. She found her bra and panties strewn on the floor, and quickly pulled them on before sitting down on the bench at the foot of his bed.

"Masaki, as you've said, I spend three to four nights of every week with you, and you spend the rest with me at my place. Even if I wanted to fuck with someone else, when would I have time? I'm not seeing anyone else. I don't want anyone else. This isn't about you. This is about me and my life. It's about…"

The muffled ringing of her cellphone interrupted her her. She jumped up to get it, abandoning the conversation to answer the line.

She swiped right on the phone screen, and put it to her ear.

"Speak," she answered.

"We've got a problem. You're needed."

With no further response, she ended the call and grabbed her clothing scattered around the room.

"You are not leaving this conversation, Oshun. We are finishing this."

"It's already finished, Mas. I can't give you what you want. I can be with you, but I can't commit the way you want me to."

She dressed quickly, and walked down the stairs in her socked feet, grabbing her black low-top sneakers from the hall cupboard she'd placed them in when she'd arrived a few hours ago. She tied them, then turned to watch Masaki as he descended the stairs.

She didn't give him the chance to speak. She didn't have time for all that. By the sound of her partner's voice on the other end of her cellphone, things were about to get messy. But then again, things were always messy in her life.

That call served as a perfect reminder of why she could never commit to a man like Masaki Yamaguchi. Everything from the way he dressed, combed his hair, and even the way he furnished his house, denoted how organized and compartmentalized his life was. She wouldn't wreck his neat and clean life just to smear it with the grimy filth that plagued hers. Even though she knew he probably wouldn't agree, she cared too much to bring this baggage to his doorstep.

She kissed him quickly, then slipped through the door as she called over her shoulder, "I'll call you later today."

A chill spilled down her spine as she walked to her car, and thoughts of doubt began to plague her. "Hopefully he still answers when I call."

2

Masaki slammed the front door and ran back up to his bedroom. He paced quickly back and forth across the large room, trying his best to quiet the rage bubbling in his head.

He'd tried hard to keep his other life away from Oshun, but Masaki couldn't allow himself to be pushed around by anyone, not even the soulful beauty who'd captivated him these last three months.

He knew he couldn't force Oshun to be with him if she didn't want to be, but he could damn sure get answers as to why. Answers he'd been seeking since he'd first connected with Oshun three months ago.

He could remember that first night so clearly in his mind. He'd seen the vixen with locs or rather he'd seen the treacherous way she'd swayed her hips to the vibrant rhythms of Erykah Badu's, "Danger," blasting through the club's speakers. He watched the intricate sensual way she'd danced, and his cock chubbed up at first glance.

He remembered listening to that song, thinking how sexy she was, and how complicated trying to be with a man like him would be for someone so full of life. Three months later, irony had thrown in an unexpected twist. Although he was the one with the "complex occupation," his waitress lover was the one who seemed to pose the relationship complications.

Masaki had known from the first a relationship between them wouldn't be wise, or easy. In his line of work, it never was. He'd been in this scenario before, seen a beautiful woman, and wanted her. Usually, that brief blip of interest waned, and he continued with his day as planned. But, Oshun had been different from the start.

Not one to be driven by his physical desires, yet Masaki took notice of Oshun, and set about securing her company for the evening. He'd watched her travel back to her seat at a booth in the VIP section once she'd finished dancing.

He'd stood at the bar, then asked the bartender to send her whatever she was drinking and put it on his tab. When she had the drink in hand, she held the glass up to him in salute, and motioned for him to come join her behind the velvet rope.

Sitting there talking to her had been an exercise in patience. He'd wanted nothing more than to find somewhere they could get naked for a few hours, there he could skeet off a nut or two and then be on his way. But, chatting for just those few minutes with the thirty-two-year-old young woman kept him enchanted long enough to remain seated next to her. Her chocolate brown eyes cued him into her keen wit, something even sexier than her cinnamon brown skin, high round tits, and ample ass.

"I love your dreadlocks," were the first words he'd spoken to her. She smiled, leaning into him as she ran her fingers through her hair.

"Honey, there's nothing dreadful about my locs. They're locs, not dreadlocks. And they're beautiful, just like me."

The fire he'd felt when she'd educated him about the state of her hair, made him burn with need. Her confidence wasn't an act or a game. It was refreshing, just one more thing about her entire package that kept him seated next to her.

They'd both known from that first drink, hell, from the first few words they'd spoken, that they would end up fucking before the night was through. She'd been game with his plan, made no qualms about it, asked for no pretenses to be offered. She wanted to fuck, and she was all-in for allowing him to spend the night pleasing her. When they'd arrived at the hotel, she'd made it clear she wasn't looking for anything but some fun. She didn't want to exchange numbers, didn't want to know anything about him other than if he had enough condoms to last the night. Hearing her stipulations, he'd been certain he'd found the perfect companion for the evening.

It wasn't until the morning when he'd awoken to an empty bed, his dick damn-near raw from all the fucking they'd done, that he realized he'd made a terrible mistake. Letting that woman go without being able to contact her quickly became a regret he couldn't live with.

It had taken him a month of showing up at the club under the cover of having a good time to, "accidently" run into her again. She was serving customers drinks in the same VIP lounge he'd met her in. It didn't matter to him that she was a waitress. He wasn't interested in what she did for a living, only that she'd allow him to spend time with her. The memory of what it felt like to be buried so deeply inside her made him determined she wasn't getting away. He wouldn't relent until he'd convinced her a friends-with-benefits scenario was a workable way for them to enjoy each other and avoid the entanglements of being in a committed relationship.

He'd thought he was so smart in convincing her to go

along with his plan. Too bad he hadn't calculated the fact he would become attached to more than just the sex, but to the woman as well.

Until this moment, they'd kept their lives separate, living in the now. But knowing she was holding back on him, especially when he suspected it was because of another man, didn't sit well with him.

If she wanted to run game, she'd chosen the wrong man to do it with. The power and connections he possessed always swayed things in Masaki's favor. Crossing him wasn't a smart thing to do. So, as much as he cared for her, if she wanted to act like a trick, he'd treat her like any other toy he'd possessed. He'd stake his claim, letting her and everyone else know there was a hefty penalty for touching what belonged to him.

He went looking for his phone when he heard it chirping on his nightstand. He picked it up, waiting for the caller to speak.

"Boss, we've got a problem."

Every time Masaki heard the word "Boss" his brain shifted gears, and the transformation began. Most days, Masaki wore the face of a clean cut real estate developer. He wore crisp button-down shirts, silk ties knotted to perfection with creased suits sharply tailored to fit only him. It was all a persona developed to prevent anyone who watched him too carefully from seeing the truth of who he really was; the head of the Canarsie Yakuza family.

Could this night fuck with my nerves anymore?

His second, Izumitani "Izzy" Hisato, was supposed to be in the middle of a high-priority job Mas had delegated to him. This call instantly pulled Mas from the day-to-day facade he wore for the public and Oshun, and made him sink into the ruthless gangster his organization demanded he be.

"Where are you?" Mas tucked the phone between his ear

and shoulder, picking up the shorn clothes Oshun had pulled off him a few hours ago.

"Mother Gaston & Hegeman."

Masaki ran down the stairs and slipped his feet into his shoes.

"On my way now."

Masaki opened his door, and took the few steps to the driveway. A few moments ago, he was making love to his woman and asking her to move in with him. Knowing Oshun would balk at being called his woman, his mood soured more. Her skittish ass might be afraid of commitment, but he wasn't. She was his, and he was hers. In his mind, there was no other alternative than for them to be together. All that remained was for him to convince her of that.

But first, he had to deal with whatever this shit was that Izzy was calling him about.

"One problem at a time, Masaki," he whispered to himself. "One at a time."

Oshun shifted carefully through the massive crowd behind the NYFD barricade as she looked for one face in particular. At six-feet-two, Aesop Jenkins stood above most people in the crowd by at least a head. When she spotted his signature light Caesar haircut, cedar complexion, and the faithful toothpick he kept trapped between his full lips, she made her way toward him.

She said nothing when she found him. There were too many people around for her to express her thoughts openly. Not to mention, with all the emergency vehicles and their wailing sirens, there wasn't much chance of being heard anyway.

Her lips tightened into a flattened line as she squinted and assessed the blackened destruction of the now-extinguished fire. The row of attached two family houses on Mother Gaston Boulevard were now gaping holes of charred brick and steel. An entire block of buildings was gone in an instant.

She wasn't angry that AAM Developing had suffered such a loss. She knew by their track record those houses were going to be used as drug dens. But, on the other side of those houses were properties owned by members of her community. People she'd promised to protect if they followed her and adhered to the rules put forth by her council. Now those people would suffer along with AAM, and she couldn't have that.

"Club, now," was all she said before turning around to begin the two-block walk between the site of the fire and Heaven's Gate.

She didn't need to look behind her to know Aesop was following her. She didn't even need to hear the heavy footfalls of his workman's boots crunching hard against the concrete sidewalk. She knew he followed her, because it was his job to follow her, explicitly and implicitly.

She keyed in the alarm code and entered the doors of the darkened venue. Heaven's Gate usually brought calm to her restless soul. It was strange that a place usually filled with loud music and boisterous patrons dancing wall to wall could make her feel calm, but it did.

When she was just a club owner, her soul was at rest. It was rare when she didn't have to worry about making certain her community was protected from all threats, that her people were thriving in a system that set them up for failure from birth. But tonight, even inside these hallowed walls, there was no peace.

She headed for the basement, not surprised to see the

lights were already on when she opened the door. She took purposeful steps down the staircase, and catalogued each face sitting at the rectangular table in the center of the room.

Big Craig, Chelly, and Uncle Pete ran the prostitution, the gambling, and chop shop rackets on the north side of Brownsville. Oshun controlled the money laundering and protection rings on the south side. With more money from her enterprise, and a larger piece of the territory under her control, Oshun sat at the head of the council. A fact that hadn't been easily accepted at first, especially by their eldest member, Uncle Pete. However, over time, they each saw her as a worthy leader who kept them paid, and paid people made happy subordinates.

Oshun taught them the way to remain successful was to engage community support. If they did things that placed the community at risk, they would always have to worry about some do-gooder trying to bring them down. They needed to take care of the community, and the community would take care of them.

The first thing she implemented was a community outreach of sorts. No crime was to be perpetrated against members of the community, only against entities that would take from the community. Her council members had to protect Brownsville, and they had to put an agreed-upon percentage of their profits back into the community.

Before Oshun instituted the restricting of how hustles were run in Brownsville, it was a wasteland of death, drug addiction, and crime. Now, the community was beginning to thrive, and if it were up to Oshun, it would remain that way.

The key was organization. The community balked at prostitutes walking the streets, or women sacrificing their health as sex workers, and pimps beating and killing the girls they victimized. Oshun helped Big Craig set up brothels near the business district that only opened when the businesses closed for the day. All Big Craig's girls received regular healthcare at no cost to them, as well as took a favorable seventy-thirty split in earnings. Craig had balked about the changes in the beginning, but then the cops stopped busting his girls, and he saw his revenue increase rapidly. It was hard to argue with that logic.

When Chelly's gambling ring kept getting raided because nosey neighbors reported the undesirables hanging out on the block, Oshun formulated a plan. She turned Chelly's brick and mortar business into a virtual casino whose IP codes were damn near impossible to track. With the cost of overhead going down and the profits pouring in, Chelly happily conformed to Oshun's business model.

When legislation produced heftier penalties for grand theft auto, Oshun stepped in to help Uncle Pete restructure his hustle. Instead of stealing the cars himself, she had him contract out the work. She also had him taking on more insurance fraud cases than before. Stealing cars brought unwanted attention. Frankly, there were too many people who wanted to cash in on the insurance money when payments became too much to handle. So now, Pete didn't have to worry about breaking into and stealing cars himself. He simply designated a drop off spot with the owners, picked up the unwanted vehicles, and broke them down for parts.

Each one of her council members leveled-up when Oshun gave them a plan to run their businesses more efficiently, as well as in ways that didn't put them in opposition with the community.

Her plans always focused on minimizing risk and maximizing profit. The only thing the members had to sacrifice was violence and drugs.

It had been difficult to get them to give up their interests in guns and drugs. Getting them to police their people and penalize them for breaking council rules had been damn near impossible. But over time, these three learned times were good when they followed Oshun, and not so good when they went against her wishes.

Oshun quietly took her seat at the table, and waited for Aesop to close the door and take his place standing behind her seat.

"Someone want to tell me what happened?"

She watched the three council members gathered around the table, each directing their eyes to anywhere but where they needed to be, on her.

"Don't all speak at once," she said to the still-quiet room.

When no one spoke, she stood up, placing spread palms against the table as she braced herself. These three people had helped her bring Brownsville up out of the dark hardships that plagued communities of lower socioeconomic status.

No, it wasn't a wealthy haven overflowing with milk and honey. But, with hard work, Brownsville had become a working-class neighborhood. The council initiated programs geared to teach skills to the unemployed and undereducated. They'd sponsored grants designed to place competitive tools in their schools, and provided opportunities for residents to attend college, and start businesses within the community. They were doing good work. Brownsville was still on the come-up, but at least they were moving in the right direction. Tonight was the first time in her ten-year reign she worried all her work could be undone.

"What the fuck happened? As far as I understand it, the plan was for us to sneak in and fuck up their shit enough to cause code violations for the inspectors coming in a few days. How the fuck did we jump from that to burning down their fucking buildings, along with the neighboring houses owned by our damn people?"

Uncle Pete, an older man who was an original gangster

from when her father was running Brownsville, finally turned his gaze to hers. He still wore wool fedoras or Bermuda hats wherever he went. He took a pull from the cigar resting between the thick pointer and ring finger of his right hand.

"It wasn't part of the plan, Oshun. Shelly, Craig, and me put some of our best people on the job. Aesop oversaw it all. Them damn Yakuza was waiting on them when they got there."

She turned to Aesop, her right hand, for confirmation of the old man's version of events.

"They ambushed us," Aesop said as he nodded his head. Just as we were finishing up, they caught us. There was a struggle between one of them and Craig's people while he was messing with the wiring. A light broke, and the fire started. We barely made it out alive."

She digested Aesop's comments, turning them over repeatedly in her mind. There was something picking at the back of her mind that didn't sit right with her. They'd watched this site for more than a month to get AAM's pattern down. They'd known everything about their security and had planned this job accordingly. Oshun wasn't sloppy, and she didn't allow her people to be either. Something was wrong here.

"How the fuck did they know we were coming?"

Again, everyone sitting at the table remained quiet.

"Someone talked," she answered her own question. "That's the only way they could've found out about our plan. Find out who the fuck is telling tales. We reconvene in two days. By then, y'all silent asses better have answers for me."

She stepped away from the table, walked up the stairs and out of the club. Her anger turned to breathtaking pain when she glanced at the burned ruins marking her failure to keep her promise to her people.

The sadness cloaking her soul weighed heavily on her, pulling her into a sinking pit of despair and disappointment as she stood there trying to figure out how she was going to fix this. The easy fix was to help her neighbors rebuild. That would take some of the burden off, but she knew it wouldn't repair the parts of their spirits that were destroyed with their mementoes, and memories that often colored the places a person called home.

"Oshun?"

She turned around at the familiar voice calling her name. It was out of place, somehow not fitting properly into her surroundings.

"Masaki? What are you doing here?"

It seemed like hours since she'd left him standing pissed off at his front door. A quick glance at her watch told her only forty-five minutes had elapsed. Did he follow her? Did he track her down to this site? She shook her head, trying to loosen the discomfort those thoughts brought to her.

He couldn't have followed you. You would've noticed a tail. But how and why was he here?

"One of my employees called to alert me of the fire. What about you?"

"I know many of the people who live in this area. I needed to come down and see how bad it was. Needed to see if there was any way I could help."

It wasn't a complete lie. It was mostly true. Yes, she did know the people who'd lost their homes. But Masaki didn't know about the true nature of her ties to the club. He didn't know she was the owner, and he damn sure didn't know about her connection to the underground council that, until tonight, protected Brownsville from all threats.

She replayed his words in her mind on a loop until something clicked in her head. "Did you say one of your employees called you?"

He nodded. "Yeah."

"Why would a real estate agent need to know about a fire that ravaged houses that weren't for sale?"

"Because my development company owns the properties on the other side where the fire began."

"You work at AAM Development?"

He shook his head. "No," he answered. "I own it."

Little more than an hour ago she was laying in his bed, quivering with need, falling victim to the pleasure he expertly doled out. Now, she was standing in the wake of the destruction she'd helped unleash on her own people. And worse yet, the man she'd been so captivated by for the last three months was part of what had led her down this dark path.

Dear God, I'm sleeping with the enemy.

3

Oshun sat in front of her computer watching as each line of info she scrolled climbed up the screen. She wasn't the greatest hacker in the world, but she knew enough to get the information she was looking for.

Birth records, social security number, citizenship, educational documents, professional licenses, and property listings was some of the information she'd been able to get so far. Masaki Yamaguchi's life was spread out for her inspection on the large computer screen. Now, she just had to dissect it and piece it all together to make sense of the confusion in her head.

Everything was as Mas had told her. He was born in Tokyo, Japan, immigrated with his parents to the States when he was a toddler, spent his life living in Canarsie with his parents, and owned AAM Developing.

Oshun rubbed the side of her temple, trying to stave off the headache she could feel creeping up behind her eyes. This was outrageous. How could everything come back so clean if he was in bed with the Yakuza?

He lived in a simple two-family home in Canarsie, Brooklyn that he'd converted into a duplex. He was a product of public education. He wore a suit and tie to work every day. He was clean, maybe too clean.

She allowed memories of their union over the last three months to play in her head. Nothing about their time together pointed to anything screaming a Yakuza connection.

He doesn't even have full body tattoos.

She allowed her mind to conjure up the image of him naked. She took a deep breath to remind herself this wasn't about pleasure, this was about the survival of her organization and her community.

Tanned skin, smooth to the touch with very little body hair. His chest, was strong and carved, and his arms...

"Oh, my God! His arms."

She was right, he didn't have the extensive full-body tattoos Yakuza members were notorious for. However, he did have full-sleeve tattoos on each arm.

She pressed harder against her temple as she remembered a distinct conversation they'd had about his tats. The first night they'd slept together, she'd noticed them, noting how strange it was to find them on a man who looked so pristine. He'd laughed, telling her they were a result of rebellion against his father, and the life his father had planned for him.

It was a perfectly fitting answer; one she never questioned until this moment. Now that she knew he was the owner of AAM, she wasn't certain if Masaki's answer felt as true as it once had.

Dull vibrating against her desk pulled her eyes away from the computer and down to her phone. Masaki's name flashing across the screen made the bottom of her stomach twist into an uncomfortable knot. She slid her finger left, sending the call to voicemail.

She'd been ducking him since the fire. That was a week ago. A week of gaining access to government databases and sorting through all the information she'd procured, yet she still didn't have a definitive answer. Was Masaki involved with the Yakuza, or wasn't he?

Nothing in the documents presented a clear picture. Nothing definitively said, "Yes, I belong to an evil, criminal organization that is trying to destroy your community."

Determined to find what she was looking for, she delved back into the data on her screen, scouring it once again in hopes of either vindicating Masaki, or convicting him. This middle ground filled with uncertainty and doubt was an uncomfortable place she refused to dwell.

If Masaki was mixed up in the Yakuza, he'd go down with them. It wasn't a choice she wanted to have to make. In fact, she desperately wanted this all to be some crazy misunderstanding.

Though she'd never admit it to him, Masaki had become someone important to her. He wasn't just a fuckboy she'd picked up at the club. The truth was, even though that's what she'd told herself all the time, she'd been in denial about how strongly she felt for the man. She'd allowed herself to believe her only interest in him was the sex. The way her heart leapt when he'd asked her to move in completely destroyed any idea that their connection was only about their sex. Your heart didn't dance when an insignificant fuck buddy asked you to commit.

Sadness filled her as she pondered what all the latest developments meant for them. She'd known soon enough she would have to walk away. Him giving her keys to his place, asking her to move in, was the beginning of the end for them. But, even though she'd sensed the end approaching, she hadn't thought she might have to bring harm to Masaki if they went their separate ways. A connection with the Yakuza meant there'd be no amicable parting. This would mean war, and war was always bloody.

A loud banging on the door made her jump to her feet and focus her attention toward the foyer. The sound repeated itself, making her reflexes kick into overdrive. She reached in the drawer of her desk to remove her pistol. She cocked it, and flipped the safety off.

The loud thumping kept rumbling against the door. She stepped quietly and carefully toward the sound. A brief peek at the security monitors on the nearby hall table showed an animated Masaki banging on her door with such force she could feel the vibrations through the floor.

Securing her gun behind her back, she called out through the door, "What do you want?"

"Open the door, Oshun! We need to talk."

She took a deep breath, hoping the added oxygen would force her brain to stop thinking of how tasty he looked in his tight black t-shirt. The fabric was stretched so tightly across his muscled chest, it was difficult to focus on how she was going to resolve this situation.

"Mas, today isn't a good day. I really need to be alone."

She anticipated more yelling to accompany the anger that had him pounding his fist against her door only moments before. What she received instead was soft-spoken concern that unnerved her more than the violent banging had.

"Oshun, I've been worried sick about you. The last I saw you was the night of the fire. You haven't answered one of my calls since then. Please, just talk to me, baby. Tell me what's wrong."

The sound of concern in his voice reminded her of how gentle he always was with her. He always sought to take care of her, meet her needs. It grieved her that her connection to the council had never allowed Oshun to reciprocate in kind.

"Watashi no megami, watashi ni hanashite kudasai."

God, this man knew her weaknesses. Her mind raced with so many tender moments they'd shared. They were all filled with him working beyond her rough exterior by sharing his heritage with her.

It seemed silly, him speaking to her in Japanese, or him making her traditional Japanese meals shouldn't have impacted her so greatly. But every time he did, it was as if he were sharing something so special about himself that she couldn't help but feel proud he'd chosen to expose himself to her.

In their three months together, he'd taught her enough Japanese that she could pick up parts in a conversation to understand general meaning. That phrase specifically, he'd used it consistently when he was attempting to get her to share herself with him.

My goddess, please talk to me.

She remembered the first time he'd spoken those words. She'd asked him why he'd referred to her as a goddess. His response, *"I didn't call you 'a' goddess, but 'my' goddess. Mine because that's how I see you, and goddess because Oshun was an African goddess."*

It shocked her that he'd known anything about the history of her name. It shocked her even more that he cared enough to learn it on his own without any prodding from her.

Hearing him appeal to the soft spot he knew she had for him made Oshun replace the safety on the gun, and slide it behind the security monitors on the table before she unlocked the door and opened it.

"Mas, calling me your goddess isn't going to fix this."

He walked past her, heading directly for her living room. If she'd been smart, he wouldn't even know what her living room looked like. But, she'd allowed herself to fall so deeply under his spell, she'd permitted him in her home within a month of them meeting. Now, he was comfortable enough in her place that he didn't need her to escort him to any part of it. Yet another mistake on her behalf she'd have to try to rectify.

"Oshun, you don't just get to forget about me. Not without some sort of explanation anyway."

His anger evident by the narrowed slits of his eyes and his squared shoulders held up by his hands positioned on either side of his waist. He was angry, but there was a control to his anger that made her reasonably certain he wasn't there to hurt her.

She shook her head quickly. A week ago, she wouldn't have thought it possible for Mas to hurt her. But, now that she knew there might be some connection between him and her enemies, she'd be a fool not to consider his ability to bring harm to her.

"I'm not sure what you want me to say, Mas. I told you when we started this I wasn't looking for anything serious. I'm sorry if the time we spent together made you think otherwise. Moving in together isn't something I can do."

He folded his arms across his chest, widened his stance, and licked his lips.

"So, you going ghost is all about the fact that I want you to be more than a piece of ass to me?"

She dropped her eyes to the floor as she nodded her head. Oshun knew full well she was more than just a sex partner to Masaki. He treasured her; it was evident in the way he expertly played her body with the simplest of touches. It was glaringly obvious in the ways he took care of her outside of bed, cooking for her, and showering her with attention and affection whenever they hid behind the walls of each other's homes.

He stepped closer to her, using his finger to lift her chin, ensuring her gaze was locked on him.

"You don't believe this bullshit you're spewing. You may not say it Oshun, but, we both know I wasn't the only one entangled in this thing between us."

He dug his fingers through her locs, pulling her mouth to his, slipping his tongue inside as soon as their lips met. His right hand moved deftly up the side of her hip and around her waist, pulling her abruptly against him.

She tried not to crumble, well, at least that's what she told herself in her head. But the truth was as soon as his lips touched hers, she was willing to do just about anything Masaki wanted.

He removed his hands from her hair and waist, moving them to the front of her button-down top. While his mouth still devoured hers, he pulled the top apart, letting his eager hands cup her lace-covered breasts. He ran his thumbs across her nipples, smiling against her mouth at the shiver he felt pass through her.

When his touch elicited a deep moan of satisfaction from her, he pulled his mouth away from hers. Securing his hands under her arms, he pulled her up until her legs were wrapped around his waist.

He walked them to her bedroom, laying her gently across the cool white linens beneath her. He pushed away from her, briefly taking the inviting warmth of his body with him as he reached for a condom in her nightstand drawer.

He didn't bother undressing them. He pulled his pants down far enough to pull out his thickening cock and sheath it. He lifted her skirt, and pushed her panties aside with two probing fingers, checking to see if she was ready for him.

The slide of his digits in and out made her walls weep and contract, begging to be filled with something meatier than the lone finger he was using.

She was too turned on to care about how desperate she looked with her legs spread, humping his fingers, begging him for more. Oshun slid her fingers between her lips, swirling them over her sensitized nub.

"You have no idea how much I love watching you touch yourself. How much it turns me the fuck on to watch you get yourself off."

Yes, she did. As much as she enjoyed masturbating on her own, watching his dark eyes sparkle with desire as he watched her pleasure herself made cumming by her own hand a favorite pastime.

He removed his fingers from her cunt, and waited for her to replace them with her own. She slid her hand under her thigh and inserted one finger inside. She was wet, slick with need, making the one finger slide effortlessly in and out of her. When the single digit wasn't enough, she added another and moaned at the electric sensation of being penetrated.

Fucking herself on two fingers of one hand while rubbing her swollen clit with the other had her passion cresting. She was about to fall over the edge just as he pulled her fingers out of her and slammed his cock into her.

The feel of his domed cap rubbing against her happy spot in perfect rhythm made her come apart. She could feel her muscles tightening with each squirt of her release. She couldn't worry about how soaked her sheets would be when they were done. The way he was fucking her, pulling each wave of her orgasm from her, her brain couldn't muster enough give a damn to worry about anything else other than how good she felt cumming on his cock.

When her legs were quivering from the last shocks of her orgasm, Masaki leaned over, pounding into her, wearing her slick walls out, pushing her over into another orgasm as he reached his own.

When his rhythm faltered, and she felt the swell of his cockhead inside her, she contracted her walls, milking him of his release, the way he'd taken hers.

When he was done, he leaned over, kissing her so sweetly it made her ache for more. He looked into her eyes, chest still heaving from their rigorous fucking, and his breath still a struggle to control.

"What we do," he gasped. "This isn't just about sex."

He pulled out, removed the condom and tossed it into the wastebasket beside the bed. He laid back down, pulling her into his arms, holding her head against his chest.

"Don't run from us, Oshun. Give me the chance to show you what we could be if we only tried."

Too tired and satiated to fight, she simply nodded her head, snuggling closer to him. She kept her eyes closed until his even breathing assured her he was asleep.

She untangled their limbs carefully, then set about removing her disheveled clothing, and pulled a long t-shirt from her closet. Once it was on, she quietly stepped out of the room, closing the door with a soft click. She picked up her cellphone from her desk, and walked out onto the balcony of her living room, closing the sliding door behind her.

Her second answered on the first ring. "What do you need?" Aesop's question was a loaded one. She needed the man in her bed to not be involved in the middle of this mess she'd found herself in. She needed to be able to care for him without dread looming over her head.

Unfortunately, she couldn't tell her friend that. Instead she decided to end this shit as quickly as possible. She'd sacrificed her life to the game. But for some reason, she wasn't inclined to sacrifice the connection she shared with Masaki so easily.

Call it love, call it lust, but whatever it was had a hold on her. Enough of a hold that she worried about their ability to survive the hell they'd find themselves in.

"Set up a meeting with the other side. The leader, 'Sop. He

and I are gonna figure this shit out. I want this done. Brownsville almost burned to a crisp last week. We've gotta find some middle ground quick before there are more casualties."

"I'll get back to you when I have something in place."

She ended the call and took a deep breath. Brownsville couldn't suffer any more than it had. And maybe if she settled this shit, she could find a way to keep Masaki out of all of this. Maybe she could find a way to keep him in her life too.

4

Masaki stood at the window in his Flatlands Avenue office, looking at the passing traffic. Watching the blur of vehicles pass one by one calmed him, keeping him settled enough to piece his thoughts together.

"Boss, did you hear me?"

Masaki nodded his reply to a sitting Izzy. He'd heard every word his second had told him. The Brownsville Council was pushing for a summit to discuss a truce.

The balls of this council galled Masaki. They'd terrorized his operation for months, and now they thought they had enough power to bring terms to Masaki. If this call had come a week before, he would've ignored it and sent his men in on a rampage instead. But, he and Oshun had moved in together, and she needed him. Starting a war would impede his ability to be there.

She was skittish. She only brought one suitcase full of clothing with her, and she refused to put her house up for sale. He knew she was keeping it as a fall back. Her refusal to sell her home was a just-in-case-this-doesn't-work-out sort of thing. He wanted to argue it, but, he knew if he pushed, she might bolt.

He couldn't risk it. He could not give her cause to leave. More and more he noticed the pull this woman had on him. Her presence was enough to make him rethink everything in his life, including how he ran his business.

"Set up the meeting, Izzy. I want this finished," he answered, his back still facing his second-in-command as he continued to gaze out of the office window.

"You sure you want to go out like this? You give these fools a sign of weakness and they'll keep coming for you."

Masaki turned slowly, looking at the man who'd worked beside him for years. Izzy sat in one of two arm chairs facing Masaki's desk. He was leaning back, legs extended, crossed at the ankles, feet propped up on top of Masaki's large wooden desk. Izzy was comfortable, too comfortable. A fact that Masaki was noticing with greater frequency over the last few weeks.

Masaki walked over to the desk, sitting next to the spot where Izzy's feet were resting. He took one long look at Izzy's feet, and then set his gaze on Izzy. He said nothing, just watched and waited quietly. Masaki noted the moment fear and understanding took root in Izzy's eyes. The man swallowed deep, as he quickly his feet from Masaki's desk.

"It's not your job to worry about how I look, Izzy. Your job is to do what I tell you. Now, do it. Set up the meet."

Izzy nodded his head quickly and left the room. Masaki was certain an agreed upon time would be in the making. These bastards had better be grateful Oshun had come to him in the middle of this ugliness. Without her, he'd burn every inch of this neighborhood to the ground, and watch all his enemies die with the strike of a match.

Oshun's presence granted this council leniency. She worked in a club that sat in the middle of where the action was happening. A shift in wind direction, and the club could have been set aflame and reduced to ash like the private homes on Mother Gaston Boulevard.

When he'd seen her at the site of the fire, his body went numb with worry. What if she had been walking by that block on her way to work? What if she'd been visiting with some of the residents over there when the fire began. She could've been burned, or worse, killed.

A dark weight sat in his belly, spreading dread throughout his system. He would never forgive himself if anything happened to this woman on his watch.

So, if working out a truce with the Brownsville Council made him seem weak, he didn't care. The only thing he cared about was the woman who'd slept in his bed every night this week

---

"Y ou sure about this, Oshun? I don't trust these cats. What if they try something?"

Oshun sat in the passenger seat of Aesop's truck, and tried not to give his words too much weight. He was right. They could be walking into a trap. The Yakuza had demanded there be only four people at the meeting. The two leaders, and their seconds.

She knew agreeing to these terms left her vulnerable, but she couldn't think about that right now. She'd moved in with a man she couldn't completely trust until this bullshit was settled.

She'd told herself the best way to find out anything was if she was on the inside. She knew she was lying to herself even as she allowed those words to cross her thoughts. The truth was she could watch Masaki better from her current vantage point as cohabitant, but, if she were honest, she was there because being with him soothed her in a way she hadn't experienced in quite a long time.

She'd opted out of dating a few years back, realizing there was no room for outsiders in her world. Being with her would only frustrate a man because she couldn't share her life, or it could place him in danger because he shared ties with her. These decisions were exercises in frustration she just didn't need, so she'd stuck to one-off hook-ups. A decision she could happily say worked very well for her until she encountered Masaki.

All her instincts told her entangling herself with him was a bad idea. But losing him, losing the way he always made her feel wasn't something she was ready to do.

Growing up as the daughter of a gangster, being taught from the very beginning that you did what was necessary to get what you needed and wanted, she knew she didn't deserve the kind of attention and affection Masaki bestowed on her. When your hands were covered in blood, when you had no qualms with taking a life, or indulging in the underworld as a means of survival, you didn't deserve the kindness Masaki covered her with.

She knew she didn't deserve it. But, she wasn't about to let it slip through her fingers either. She was selfish, but that was nothing new. She wouldn't apologize for it either.

Instead, she'd move forward with this treaty between the two factions. Hopefully, it would bring this pending war to an end, and her people, as well as her heart would be safe from the threat currently looming over their heads.

"I know that, 'Sop." She rubbed her hand at the base of her neck, attempting to rid it of the tension building as they neared the meeting spot on Linden Boulevard and Seventy-Eight Street.

"The diner has always been neutral ground, but there's only one way in and out of it. I don't know if I like it."

It was true. The diner at the end of Linden had always been considered a hands-off place. You could eat and drink with your crew, but no hustling could take place on the premises. Most factions adhered to that. Unfortunately, the Yakuza hadn't been in the area long enough for her to determine if they'd play by the established rules or not.

Aesop slowed down, pulling into the dim parking lot of the diner. She opened her door, and walked around to where Aesop stood on the driver's side.

"'Sop, we don't have time to worry about all that."

She grabbed the handle of her gun making sure it was secure in the holster attached to the back of her pants. Satisfied it was fastened, she pulled down the loose shirt she wore to cover the metal bulge.

"You got your piece. I got mine. If some shit pops off, we handle it, just like we always do. You and I have tamed this land. Ain't no way we can't get this newbie on the scene under control. You wit' me?"

Aesop nodded his head and lead the way up the few steps to the diner. To anyone on the outside looking in, Aesop appeared to be an inconsiderate fuck walking ahead of his girl. In reality, he was clearing a path for her, making certain no harm met her before it met him.

When he was reasonably certain the walkway didn't possess an ambush, he opened the door, stepped through it, and then held it open for her to do the same. Once inside, he followed the hostess to the private room in the back, and Oshun kept pace behind him.

Once inside the private dining room, she continued to

stand behind Aesop. When he deemed it safe, she'd step from behind him and walk to their target.

An Asian man, a head shorter than Aesop, stood in front of her companion and talked for a brief moment. Aesop turned around, still crowding her in the small doorway and pointed to her.

"Oshun, this is Izzy. Izzy, Oshun."

The man wore dark shades inside the dimly lit room. She wondered if he could even see out of those sunglasses. He dipped his head in acknowledgement of the introduction before turning his back to them. He beckoned them with a curled finger.

He walked them through another door, toward a table in the back of the room. When they finally came to a halt, the human wall Izzy and Aesop created in front of her parted, and allowed her to lay eyes on the lone man sitting at the table.

Familiar full lips, tanned skin, and coal eyes stared back at her, making her heart race with a thickened mixture of anger and fear.

"Oshun," she heard Aesop's voice calling through her loud heartbeats pounding in her ears. "This is Masaki, the leader of the Canarsie Yakuza family."

She watched as Aesop extended a hand to the man, giving him a friendly dap before continuing his introduction. "Masaki, this is the leader of the Brownsville Council, Oshun."

There was an awkward silence in the room. Neither of them saying a word, their eyes locked on one another, forgetting about their business companions who were now standing on either side of Oshun.

"Izzy, 'Sop," Masaki called to the two men standing beside her, but kept his eyes fixed on hers. "Please leave the lady and I to discuss things amongst ourselves."

Aesop leaned down and whispered quietly in her ear, "You wit' it?"

She nodded, giving him permission to take his leave. Aesop stood still next to her, looking back and forth between she and Masaki.

"I promise no harm will come to her in my company, 'Sop."

With that, Aesop took his leave. She remained standing in front of the table uncertain of what to say. She'd never wanted to find this, had given herself every excuse in the book for why Masaki's company would be involved with the Yakuza. All the excuses except for the one answer sitting in front of her now.

"I guess I understand now why you gave me such a hard time about moving in."

She yanked the chair out from under the table, and sat down in it.

"Was this a setup all along? Were you playing me this whole time? Was this just about taking over my community?"

He leaned forward quickly, planting his forearms on the table as he glared at her.

"If I had known who you were...," his voice trailing off, leaving her to wonder what the other end of that thought was. Would he have walked away from her? Could he have? She'd been trying to loosen his hold on her since they'd met three months ago. Would it have been so easy for him to cut his losses and move on?

"This was not my doing, Oshun. I didn't know, but I have a feeling you did. You've been jumpy as hell since I found you at the scene of the fire. You even attempted to cut me loose. Was it because you knew who I was?"

She shook her head. "I suspected you had some kind of involvement with the Yakuza when you told me you owned AAM. I thought they might be using you for a front. I didn't think you were actually running the damn organization."

They sat quietly in their chairs, both seeming at a loss for the right words to deal with this situation.

"What do we do now, Masaki? How do we move on from here?"

She was proud of the even control of her voice. It surprised her. If he could sense the tremors cresting and crashing on her insides, he'd have known how afraid she really was.

This man could ruin her and her community. The worst part was she'd given him the ammunition.

"I can't let you destroy my community by bringing drugs and violence back into its borders."

"I don't know what the hell you're talking about," he snapped. The sharp tone forced her to focus on him, instead of the mounting apprehension swirling in her gut. "I don't deal in the drug trade. It's too risky, and the officials I have in my pocket wouldn't be able to remain loyal to me if I dealt in drugs."

She assessed him carefully, hoping to see if she'd learned enough about him to know when he was lying or not. His eyes were focused steadily on hers, his words were direct, and his breath even.

He wasn't lying.

Then what the hell is this all about?

"Oshun, drugs are not my family's business."

"What exactly is your family's business then?" Her question drew a crooked smile from him, making her pulse quicken. Here they were, engaged in a conversation that could impact the lives of thousands, and he still found the time to be so damn sexy it made her blood bubble with desire.

"That's something only family should know. Don't you think?"

She eased back in her chair, attempting to process the unfolding events. She'd somehow missed the fact that her lover was the head of an enemy faction, and now the reason she thought they were about to go to war seemed nonexistent. None of this made much sense.

"If I'm to be completely honest, Masaki," she answered, "I don't know what to think."

5

"None of this is making sense to me either, Oshun." She felt his gaze weigh on her as he watched her stand up and slip into a smooth rhythm, pacing back and forth. He stood up and fell into rhythm alongside her as he continued the conversation. "I can't speak for Aesop, but Izzy has been loyal to me, and to my family, since we were kids. You on the other hand have been lying to me since you met me."

His words and proximity halted her motion, making her tilt her head back slowly to gaze up at him. She'd always loved the fact he was taller, his wide shoulders and chest making her feel protected and secure every time he held her. But, standing here now, the near-closed slits of his eyes coupled with the flat line of his mouth made her tremble with a strange mixture of fear and desire.

Get your shit together, Oshun. This is your territory. You are Brooklyn born, Brooklyn strong. No man can take that from you.

Committed to holding her footing in this conversation, she crossed her arms against her chest. Glaring at him, she pushed the uncertainty plaguing her down into the pit of her stomach.

"Exactly what did you expect me to say, Mas? *Hello, my name is Oshun and I run a crime syndicate that's determined to destroy yours.*"

She threw up her hands in frustration, walked away from him, and resumed her pacing. Movement helped her think, and more than ever she needed her brain power to kick in.

"I just don't buy it," he said. "Why would you move in with me when you already suspected I was involved with the Yakuza? It doesn't make sense."

His voice was distant, almost quiet. She couldn't tell if he were talking to her, or directing his question to himself. It wasn't until she turned around and saw the distinct blend of anger and hurt blazing in his eyes that she understood he wanted an answer from her.

"My intel on you came back clean. And the truth is, I wanted to believe you were clean. I wanted to forget about my business life for once and focus on how good it felt to be with you."

And it had felt good. The truth, being with Masaki, being treasured, being treated as if she were something precious and meaningful, quieted the screams of her sins in the dark of night. Being with him made her forget about the ugly blemishes on her soul.

She'd known better, but she would've done anything to keep that feeling, even lie to herself about the possibility of who Masaki was.

"I knew allowing myself to become deeply involved with you was a bad idea, but I didn't care. It didn't matter as long as I got to be with you."

She watched him step carefully toward her. When he reached her, he stood quietly looking down at her. His proximity made her uneasy. She wasn't sure if it was because he was a threat to her, or if it was because he was close enough for her to smell the woodsy fragrance of his aftershave.

The mild, but spicy aroma called to her, making her want to lean in and bury her nose in the strong curve of his neck. She shook her head attempting to clear it, but breaking free of the hold he had on her seemed impossible.

"Why would being with me matter that much to you, Oshun?" He pulled a hand from his pocket, lifting a single finger, using it to slide away an errant lock that fell over her eye. "You've fought me from day one. Why was it so important to be with me now?"

She tried to dip her head, to break free from him gaze. But, he lifted her chin with his finger, keeping their eyes locked together, demanding she answer his question.

"Because even though getting close to you was a bad idea, the thought of being without you made me ache."

He cupped his hand around the back of her neck and pulled her closer to him. The firm grip keeping her excited yet apprehensive at the same time.

You never let an enemy get this close to you. She knew this. She had the means to defend herself resting at the small of her back. But even with this knowledge, she still went willingly to him.

"You're right. This was a bad idea."

His words pulled a heavy sigh from her chest. He was right. She'd echoed those same words only moments before. However, hearing them cross his lips, hearing them from the man who'd always had endless hope where their relationship was concerned, felt like a heated, sharpened blade slicing through her heart.

She cleared her throat as she stepped away from him. Closing her eyes tightly to hold back the emotions she knew were clouding them, she took a calming breath.

"We can figure out this personal shit later, Mas. Right

now, we gotta get outta here."

"As far as I'm concerned, it's settled," he answered, making her heart sink even further inside her chest.

"Agreed," she answered. He'd made his decision, and she couldn't blame him. There was no sense in focusing on the obvious. There was no way they could continue being lovers, not with warring criminal enterprises to consider. "What's the plan now, Mas?"

He pointed to himself as he shook his head. "You're seriously asking me? You started this bullshit, and now it's my job to fix it?"

"I'm not sure what you mean, Masaki." Yes, she'd been the first to attack. But, he'd been the first to show aggression by moving into her territory without showing the slightest bit of deference to her and her people.

"You know, I extended an invitation to you months ago. I had Izzy find out the lay of the land, and he connected with your boy 'Sop. If you'd just agreed to the first meeting, where I offered you a very lucrative cut for access to your streets, none of this would've happened."

He threw his hand in the air in marked exasperation. A gesture she was finding hard to understand considering his plan had been to take over her community.

"Instead, you answered my kind gesture with an attack on my site. The shit we're in the middle of is your fault dear, not mine. It was never my intention to make this a war zone. It doesn't benefit either of us. I even extended myself again, something I don't do, just because I wanted to protect Brownsville from the bloody war you've been doing your best to start."

His words didn't make sense. He was speaking English, her native tongue, but what his words implied didn't make sense at all.

"Why would you extend my council and my people any

courtesies?" she asked. "If you didn't know I was the person on the other side of the curtain until I walked in here, why would you go out of your way to try to make peace?"

"I didn't want you to get hurt."

He sat back down at the table and motioned for her to join him. When she was seated, he leaned in across the table and gently placed his hand atop hers. The confusion she'd felt since she found him sitting in this room began to dissipate as she latched on to the truth that shone brightly in his eyes.

"I knew the club was in the hot zone. I didn't want you to wind up a casualty. So, I decided to make a deal for peace instead."

She felt herself swaying to the soft lull of comfort his hand against her skin provided. Too afraid of compromising herself further, she stood up and planted her hands firmly on the table.

"If what you say is true, Mas, something is terribly wrong. Because I never received any messages from you about peace or otherwise."

He shook his head, narrowing his eyes as he stared at her.

"That can't be possible. Izzy said he was there when 'Sop told you, and you refused."

She focused hard on his words. Something about them seemed wrong.

"'Sop? That's mighty familiar for someone you've just met."

"Just met? I've known 'Sop now since we initially broached the subject of leasing your streets. That's how I know Izzy was telling the truth about meeting with you. 'Sop was standing next to Izzy when I got the report. He confirmed everything Izzy said."

Her chest tightened, and her stomach felt as if she'd fallen twenty stories.

"Oshun, what's wrong?"

"What's wrong is I've never met Izzy before today, and I sure as hell have never had this conversation you're referring to. I don't know anything about an invitation to meet and talk business. If Aesop and Izzy say I did, they're lying."

He stood up, walking around to her side of the table. "Why would they lie?" he asked.

She pulled her gun from its holster, removed the safety, and cocked it. "I don't know," she answered. "But I'm sure as hell not sticking around here to find out."

6

Masaki pulled the weapon he'd had holstered at his back. He followed Oshun's suit, cocking his gun, and making certain he was prepared for anything that came at them.

He watched her take two steps toward the door when the room became shrouded in darkness. He pulled out his phone and tapped the flashlight app on. Once he could find Oshun in the room, he stepped in front of her, taking the lead to the door.

How had he let this happen? How hadn't he seen Izzy for the conniving son of a bitch he'd become? They'd been friends since birth, raised as brothers. How could someone he trusted so much deceive him like this?

Masaki still couldn't figure out what Izzy's end game was. What would starting a war do for him? Even if Masaki had gone to war with Oshun and the Brownsville Council, how was that supposed to benefit his second-in-command?

"It looks like our comrades have plans for us. Any idea what those plans might entail?" he asked.

Oshun remained quiet until they reached the door, shaking her head when she leaned against the door frame.

"I haven't the slightest," she answered. "I have no idea what Aesop could be after. War with you would only hurt us. Even if his plan was to take my place, he'd have to deal with the rest of the Council, and worse yet, my father."

He readjusted the angle of the phone to find the door knob.

"I can't think of a reason why Izzy would want to do this either?"

"Does he want your spot?" she asked.

"He might." He shrugged. "But he's not going to tell me that. Not to mention, taking me out doesn't guarantee he'd get top spot. I'm just the boss of this region. Any admin within the organization is hand-picked by an Oyabun, the big boss."

He watched as Oshun pointed toward the door. "Can you hear what's going on out there?"

Masaki leaned his head against the door and listened for movement. It was late when they'd entered the diner, so only a few patrons remained. He could hear the owner's distinct baritone voice directing the handful of people, made up of diners and staff still present, out of the diner, asking them to walk calmly to the illuminated exit sign.

"The owner is getting everyone out," he offered. "I don't hear many steps, there can't be but a few people out there." He went to open the door and she placed her hand on top of his, stopping him.

"They could be waiting for us to open the door."

She was right. He was certain there was some sort of ambush planned. He just had no clue what it was. This wasn't out of any playbook Masaki encountered. This was something totally new.

"I don't think Izzy and Aesop are still in the dining area.

With no windows in this private dining room, there's really no way to tell if they're still out there. But, this room is in the back, and they'd have to walk through the rest of the diner to get to us. It may be black in here, but there are windows throughout the rest of the diner. The streetlights outside would keep the diner lit enough for witnesses to see."

Oshun nodded her head. Apparently, he was making sense to her, if only any of this made sense to him.

Whatever Izzy's plan was, Masaki was going to make sure his underling lost his life before it came to fruition. He'd broken the father-son code of the Yakuza. There was no coming back from that.

"You think they're outside waiting for us?"

"That would be my guess," Masaki answered. "The parking lot is empty this time of night. Between the big windows in the diner, and the few cars in the open parking lot, there's not much coverage."

They were sitting ducks in this private dining room. They couldn't see, which meant their ability to protect themselves was jeopardized.

"All right," she said, her clipped tone pulling his attention to her. "Crack the door."

He did as she said, and watched as she crawled through the doorway on her hands and knees. Staying low to the ground was a smart move. The windows stopped at the height of the tables. If someone was outside looking in, they'd need to be elevated to see them.

He followed her, closing the door quickly behind them to prevent tipping off prying eyes. They made it to the foyer. Enclosed completely in glass, there was nowhere for them to hide. Both coming to the same silent conclusion, they stood up and readied their weapons.

The side of the parking lot they entered was isolated. There were two vehicles in the middle of it, making the open space seem larger and more daunting than ever before.

A shrill squeal of tires filled the air, placing Masaki's senses on alert. He pushed Oshun in the direction of a large SUV, and they both took off running.

As they sprinted toward the vehicle, Masaki heard bullets being fired through a suppression device somewhere in the parking lot.

Contrary to popular belief, silencers didn't actually silence firearms. They only took the firecracker bang out of them. If you were close enough, you could hear the muted thwap, thwap sound of shots being fired through the air.

Masaki heard glass shatter around them. He didn't have time to look to see what direction the bullets were coming from, he just needed to get him and Oshun behind the large SUV for cover.

Heart racing, breath coming in heavy huffs, Masaki fought to focus. He needed to figure out which direction the bullets were coming from. A quick peak around the vehicle, and he saw a flash of light coming from a sedan on Linden Boulevard.

He took another deep breath, then glanced over at Oshun, and nodded his head. She accepted his signal, and when there was a break in the curtain of bullets raining down around them, they rose just high enough to fire shots of their own.

A rapid exchange of gunfire took place. With both he and Oshun taking aim at the car, shattering the windows on the passenger side, they forced the shooter to get out of the car.

It was Izzy. The quick peak Masaki caught of him fleeing the car revealed a bloodied shoulder. It could've been from the shattered glass, but Masaki prayed that fucker had caught a bullet.

When he heard the click of Izzy's empty pistol, Masaki took the opportunity to rush toward him. Gun blazing, there was no hesitation in his trigger finger. He wished his semi was an automatic, he couldn't spray his bullets fast enough. When Izzy tried to run away from the car as Masaki closed in on him, Masaki fired a final shot and watched as it struck a running Izzy in the back of his head.

Masaki felt a twinge of celebration roll through him as he watched his target twitch and fall to the ground. He was so lost to the euphoria of vindication that he didn't hear Oshun screaming his name from behind him.

He turned around, watching her running toward him with her gun pointed to the side. He followed her line of sight to see Aesop standing with a pistol pointed in Masaki's direction.

He attempted to fire at Aesop, but there was nothing except the sound of an empty click. He was out of ammunition and standing in an open parking lot while an enemy pointed a loaded weapon at him.

He was a leader in the Yakuza. Masaki would not beg, nor would he allow fear to possess him in this moment. If this was how he met his end, he would do it with honor.

When Masaki heard the bullet leave the chamber, he held out his arms to his sides, and welcomed oblivion. His eyes were locked above him on the night sky when he felt the force knock him off his feet and onto the ground.

He blinked, waiting for the pain and burn of the bullet piercing his body. But, it never came. He felt a heaviness on top of him that forced him to pull his sight from the twinkling stars, and looked down to see Oshun lying on top of him.

He looked around for Aesop, and spotted his twitching body spasming on the ground.

"Damn woman, I'm so glad you're such a good shot."

He chuckled, expecting to hear her return his laughter, or

at the very least, rip him a new one for being so careless. But, she didn't respond.

Masaki sat up as he awkwardly attempted to get them both in an upright position. When he finally did, he called Oshun's name, but she didn't answer.

He cradled her head in his arms, and pulled her closer to him. When he pulled them apart again, he saw blood on the front of their shirts. He looked down at his chest to see where the blood was coming from. He didn't feel any pain. When he returned his gaze to Oshun's torso, the crimson stain was darker, and worse, it was spreading.

"No…no," he whispered as panic grew inside him. When his searching fingers found the oozing hole on the side of her chest, his panic turned to agonizing pain. Watching her life seep away through the bullet wound felt like a vise had been placed around his heart, squeezing and tightening until it ruptured like a damaged pipe. He'd come to this restaurant to control and destroy his enemy if necessary. He'd never conceived the idea that his enemy would save his life by sacrificing hers.

7

Masaki paced the inside of the interrogation room. Pacing was the only thing keeping him calm enough not to go on a murderous rampage. He needed out of this room in the worst way.

Oshun was hurt.

How badly, he didn't know. That fact alone was making him come unhinged. She needed him. She'd sacrificed herself to save him. Masaki wouldn't rest until he knew she was all right.

He heard the creak of the door and watched as a silver-haired Caucasian man, tall, with a slim build, dressed in an expensive dark suit, walk into the room.

"Mr. Yamaguchi," he uttered. Masaki held up his hand interrupting him before he could continue. Seth Stein was his lawyer. His legal skills had helped Masaki, and his father before him, stretch the boundaries of the law without consequence. Usually Mas would take the time to carefully listen to whatever the man advised. However, tonight's events made it impossible for Masaki to do anything but focus on Oshun.

"It's been three hours. Did you get me out of here? I need to leave."

The older man took a breath, dropped his arms to his sides, and nodded his head.

"I suppose it would be foolish of me to expect you to go home and lay low until this blows over?"

"I've never known you to be foolish, Seth."

Exasperation shone on the older man's face as he shook his head. Seth knew Masaki well enough to know when to push and when to fall back. Tonight, pushing would yield him nothing but frustration. Masaki had no intention of running and hiding. Not when Oshun needed him.

"My car is waiting outside. Where can I drop you?"

"To County General Hospital," Masaki answered. "I need to get there now."

Seth escorted Masaki out of the precinct and into his waiting car. Masaki expected a lecture, but the elder man remained quiet, leaving Masaki to his own thoughts as they traveled the short distance to the hospital.

Masaki was grateful for the silence in the car. He needed it to pull his thoughts together. He was a strategist, often thinking ten steps ahead of where he needed to be. It was how he'd expanded his father's empire so quickly. His moves were always calculated to outmaneuver his competitors. But tonight, he could barely think beyond the next second.

His thoughts were a jumble of sporadic flashes of memory. There was a glimpse of Oshun walking into that private dining room, then they were in darkness. The next frame in his mind's slideshow was the two of them running for their lives in that dark parking lot, and then Oshun slumped in his arms with a bleeding bullet wound in her chest.

Masaki snapped his eyes closed, bracing against that memory. She was limp, almost lifeless in his arms, and he'd been helpless to do anything about it except scream for help and wait for an ambulance to arrive.

He'd wanted to ride with her to the hospital, but the paramedics wouldn't let him. Instead, the cops had taken him into custody to verify his story, his gun registration, and license to carry.

Thank God he really was licensed to carry a weapon. If he weren't, he'd be behind bars right now instead of pulling up to the hospital. Fancy lawyer or not, an illegal gun charge wouldn't have been so easy to escape, even if he'd only fired it to protect himself.

When the car slowed in front of the hospital's main entrance, Masaki half turned his head toward Seth and said, "Don't tell anyone about what happened tonight. I don't know who I can trust."

Masaki swallowed the hard knowledge that someone who was supposed to be his family had betrayed him. It wasn't lost on him either that the person who was designated as his enemy, was the person who'd saved his life tonight.

The older man nodded his head in response. "The guard on duty knows you're coming in. He'll conveniently be patrolling when you walk through. The nurse will buzz you through as soon as you get to the SICU."

Masaki let out a brief sigh of relief. Having someone like Seth manipulate the system for him was a godsend. Otherwise, he'd never be able to get to Oshun.

"Her people haven't been notified of her shooting," Seth continued. "But once they have been, I don't advise you to be here. As far as they will know, your people tried to kill her. Until she can set the record straight, it might not be a good idea for you to be around when they arrive."

Seth wasn't wrong. If the Brownsville Council found him at her bedside, he was a dead man. He had no idea what, if anything, Aesop had told the rest of her crew. Hell, for all

Masaki knew, Oshun's entire organization was in on it with Aesop.

This situation was dangerous for all of them. But, he couldn't leave Oshun to brave this alone. More than that, he needed to be there for himself. If she didn't make it through this... Unwilling and unable to entertain the idea of Oshun losing this battle, he winced in reaction to the thought.

Satisfied Seth would keep the details of the shooting quiet, Masaki put his game face on, stepped out of the car onto the curb, and headed through the automatic doors of the hospital.

His passage through the security checkpoint was simple. Seth's plan was perfectly executed, and within moments, Masaki was walking through the glass doors of Oshun's surgical intensive care room.

He pulled the privacy curtain closed, then walked further inside the room, sitting in the lone chair at the side of her bed.

Her long locs were spread all over her pillow in a messy heap.

She needs her satin pillow case and head wrap. She'd never allow her hair to rub against cotton with no protection.

They'd only been together three months. It wasn't a long time. The fact that they were in this situation proved there were tons of things they still needed to learn about one another. But somehow, none of that seemed important as he stood looking down on her still body.

The way she pretended she was too hard to care about anything, but brightened whenever he did something thoughtful for her was important. The way she excitedly learned to prepare his favorite Japanese meals just to be able to surprise him with a home-cooked meal on his last birthday was important. The way she purred when he made love to her, and plastered herself against him during the night, that was important. But the rest of it, the rest of it wasn't important enough that she should be lying here with a bullet wound in her chest.

A tap on the glass sliding door pulled his attention away from Oshun. "It's Nurse Samuels. I need to check on your vitals Ms. Sampson."

She entered the room, taking care to secure the privacy curtain once the door was closed. The young nurse walked in the rest of the way, acknowledging Masaki with only a brief nod.

"How is she doing?"

The nurse didn't face him as he spoke. For the most part, she attended to Oshun, ignoring him as if he weren't there.

"I've risked enough sneaking you in here. I can't tell you anything about her condition. The only thing I can tell you is she is in serious, but stable condition."

"But she's not awake?"

"She's had a pretty exhausting day, don't you think? A girl is entitled to a little beauty rest at the end of such a long day."

She smiled at him as she was leaving, stopping once she reached the curtain again. "Don't stay too long. Her regular nurse will be returning in another thirty minutes."

The nurse disappeared behind the curtain, and slid the glass doors closed, leaving Masaki alone with an unconscious Oshun and all the beeping machines in the room. He caressed the back of her hand with careful fingers, before gently bringing it to his lips. He cradled her hand, linking their thumbs, as he closed his eyes and pressed her hand against his cheek.

"I don't know how I missed any of this, Oshun. I was so worried about fixing things to prevent you from getting hurt, I didn't see the treachery in my lieutenant's eyes. I promise you I'm going to make this right."

"You'd better," she whispered. "Otherwise us living together is going to get very complicated, very soon."

He slowly opened his eyes, hoping he wasn't conjuring up her voice. When he found heavy lidded chocolate eyes staring back at him, his fortitude crumbled, and his body shook with relieved tears.

"Are you in pain? Do you need anything?"

She squeezed his hand, as if she were lending him her strength in his weakened state. It was the nurturing side of her checking to make certain he was all right.

"I'm in pain," she answered. "But, I'm alive, so I'll deal. The bullet entered the side of my chest at an angle." She stopped, taking a slow, but deep breath before she continued again. "It tore a hole in my chest cavity. They got it out, and put a chest tube in me to keep my lung from collapsing." She paused again, drawing in another slow breath through her flared nostrils. "As long as I don't go and do something stupid like throwing a blood clot, or trying to move, I should be fine."

There she was, the young, snarky goddess he'd fallen for. The woman whose quick wit and aloofness had pulled him in that very first night he'd laid eyes on her

"When I realized you'd been shot...I thought I lost you."

She shook her head, adjusting the slipping oxygen cannula in her nose as she did. "You're not that lucky." She stopped to take another deep breath before continuing. "You gave me a key. You'd have to change the locks to get me out."

He chuckled as he stood up, placing a gentle kiss on her smiling lips. The small gesture reminding him just how lucky he was to still have her in the land of the living with him.

"I gotta tell you, I don't really see a way out of this mess for us. Izzy and Aesop set this up good. Even if your council believes I had nothing to do with this, we may still never be free of this night. I don't know who, if any, were a part of Izzy's attempted coup."

"I have the same concerns, Masaki. But." She paused another moment, holding her hand to her wounded side, taking another slow, deep breath before she attempted to speak again. "You're my enemy Masaki. Yet, my instinct was to protect you tonight. I can't ignore that." Her words warmed him from the inside. Those words calmed the raging waves of anger and fear seeing her in this condition caused. He held her hand tighter, and delighted at the weak smile pulling at her lips.

She repositioned herself in the bed, taking a moment to catch her breath as she did so. "I want you, and I'm not about to lose you to the war that's coming," she continued. "A war neither of us started."

"Oshun..." His words faded as she shook her head, holding up a lone finger in the air to silence him.

"If we're ever going to have a chance at surviving this thing as a unit, then we're going to have to figure this out together. Both our houses are in flux. Until we know how deep this deception flows, neither of us can risk letting our guards down."

For a few moments in that diner he'd doubted her. He'd doubted what they were building, he'd doubted what he felt for her, and most importantly, he'd doubted what she'd felt for him. But when she saved his life, she'd put any doubts he had to rest. He knew Oshun well enough to understand she was probably never going to be the "I love you" type. But, nearly getting herself killed to protect his life was all he needed to believe that what they shared was mutual, and deeper than any spoken declaration could ever be.

"I'm in," he answered. "Give me a few days to get things rolling. We need to get medical attention setup for you wherever we're headed."

She shook her head. "No need, arrangements for everything we need have already been taken care of. You just have to decide if you're ready to leave it all behind for however long it takes us to figure this mess out, or if you're going to walk away from us."

Walking away from her, from them, wasn't a possibility. This night had proven she would have his back harder than any of the men he employed. Letting this woman slip through his fingers wasn't an option.

Besides, he'd learned a simple fact tonight in that parking lot. They were strong independently, but together they were unstoppable. If any two people could figure this out, stop their enemies, and manage to stay alive, it was the two of them. His enemy had become his best asset, and he'd follow her into the bowels of hell.

He felt his lips curve into his signature lopsided grin; the one that danced on his lips when he needed to show the world he had nothing to worry about. And, he didn't. He was confident this partnership was going to yield great results, and the matching smile Oshun gave him from her bed, expressed the same confidence.

She'd started out being a piece he just wanted to have a good time with. She'd ended up being his peace, the other half of his gangster's soul.

Masaki leaned down over her, still smiling, until his lips pressed against hers, and he heard a relieved moan escape her mouth.

"We'll burn this motherfucker down together, Oshun. We'll kill them all."

8

M asaki waited until he thought Oshun was sleeping and released her hand, gently placing it against the white hospital sheets. She needed her rest, and he'd stayed long past the time the lurking nurse had given him. The longer he stayed, the longer he risked being spotted by the wrong person. Since neither he nor Oshun knew who the wrong person actually was, safety was more important now than it had ever been.

"You sneaking out already?"

He turned quickly at the sound of her voice and offered a smile as an answer. "You need your rest, Oshun."

She fumbled, pulling herself up slowly using the upper side rails of the bed. He stretched out his hand to stop her, but quickly realized his protest was about to fall on deaf ears.

"I will rest when we're gone."

Her words were still choppy. The chest tube, and the resulting post-op pain, made it difficult for her to speak. He wanted nothing more than to take away her pain. But since he couldn't do that, the next best thing would be to bring those responsible for her injuries to justice. His brand of justice.

"You can't exact retribution until we know who's behind this," she stated. "Rushing out there without any details will get you killed. Please, stay with me. Help is on the way."

She stretched out her hand to him, her shaky smile brightening when he clasped her hand with his and brought it to his lips. Her smile was everything to him. It was the draw of her sensual smile that had called to him across a crowded club three months ago. Tonight, her smile touched his soul with tender strokes because she was alive to share it with him. He'd accepted long ago that her smile was his undoing. As he removed his jacket and sat in the abandoned visitor's chair, he reconciled once again, he'd do whatever he had to keep that smile on her face.

"Who is this mysterious savior you keep speaking of?"

"The only person I know we can trust," she answered as she looked toward the glass door.

He followed her gaze until he saw a tall, lean African American man with similar coloring to Oshun, a warm brown with red undertones just beneath the skin. His hair was in locs too. Not nearly as long and defined as Oshun's, but they still commanded attention, letting you know you were in the presence of someone important and powerful.

"Masaki Yamaguchi, this is my father, Zion Sampson." She took another breath as she shifted her gaze to her father. "Daddy, this is Mas."

Masaki stood to offer his hand, but the man's stoic nature made Masaki think better of it. The older man took a moment to look at Masaki, then turned his attention to his daughter.

"You sure about this, baby girl?"

She nodded slowly, softening the gruff man's exterior. He returned his gaze to Masaki, and stretched out his hand in greeting. "As my daughter told you, I'm Zion Sampson. I'm the man that's going to get the both of you to safety until we figure out how to handle this."

"How soon before we leave? I'll need to collect my mother."

The older man shook his head. "You can't. If you move your mother, whoever is watching you will know. Oshun will be moved tonight. If you're going, you've got to move too."

"But my mother…"

Masaki felt a squeeze to his hand that drew his attention down to Oshun. "On my life, I promise you no harm will come to your mother. My father will protect her as if she were me."

Her assurance quieted the uncertainty floating around in his chest. She gave him the hope he needed to believe that they would all come out of this ugly scenario safely. He nodded his acquiescence to the older man, and relented to Zion's plans.

"She's my only living parent, Mr. Sampson. Please, keep her safe."

"Do the same for my baby girl and everything will turn out fine," Zion answered as he pulled a small pad of paper from his inside jacket pocket. "Write down your mother's information, then give me your phone or any electronic devices you have with you. We're going old school for this one. Completely off the grid."

9

Oshun stood in front of the mirror inspecting her healed wounds. Six weeks later, the once smooth skin that she took pride in lathering every night with coco butter, was replaced by raised lines where the surgeon's scalpel had cut. No amount of moisturizer would conceal the scar. For the rest of her life, she would be marked by the events of that night at the diner.

She heard a slight tap against her door, and quickly pulled her shirt down into place. She knew her need to conceal her wound from Masaki was silly. He'd been there when she was shot. He'd changed her bandages and taken care of her after the private physician left every night. Masaki knew what the jagged marks on her flesh looked and felt like. Strangely, as her ability to walk and independently take care of her own needs grew, so did her shame about those marks.

"Come in," she called as she smoothed the cotton fabric of her t-shirt down, and faced the door.

"I made breakfast." Masaki stepped inside, watching her carefully as she stood in the middle of her room. "You okay?"

She nodded her head and watched him respond in kind,

as he stepped back and closed the door behind him. This had become their usual. This awkward dance of not knowing what to say for fear of crossing some imaginary boundary. It was as if learning the truth about the other's identity had imprisoned them in this unnatural habitat of nice that neither of them dared to rail against.

Wasn't the truth supposed bring freedom?

Apparently, that was a lie. She'd never felt more caged than the moment she'd learned Masaki Yamaguchi, her lover, was the head of the Canarsie Yakuza.

She took a deep breath and headed for the kitchen. No need in delaying the uncomfortable meal they would have. Getting it over with so she could get on to the next awkward communication between the two of them seemed like as good a way as any to start her day.

Up until six weeks ago, she'd been a boss, the leader of the Brownsville Council. She'd been ruthless and exacting in her dealings with anyone who crossed her the wrong way. Fear had no place in her life until Masaki showed up.

Masaki, the man she'd run from in a failed attempt to protect him from her lifestyle, was her enemy. Too bad he'd never needed protection. She chuckled at that realization. Oshun had managed to avoid dangerous entanglements until she'd met Masaki. But now, things were messier than she could've imagined. Not only had she fucked around and slept with the leader of her most notorious rival yet, she'd also managed to care about him too.

Her life was a comedy of errors as of late. One moment her path was clear and definitive, the next, she was standing in front of a mirror wondering how to be herself again. She needed to figure out how to regain enough of her confidence so she could navigate this emotional land mine she and Masaki were carefully stepping through.

She took one last look at herself in the mirror, running

her fingers through the intricate twists of her brown locs with the chestnut tips.

"You have no choice but to hide in this house until the two of you come up with a plan. You will not be complicit in hiding from Masaki too. Get your shit together, Oshun. You can do this."

Once she made it downstairs, she found Masaki in the kitchen holding two coffee mugs in one hand and a coffee pot in the other. He smiled when he saw her, easing some of the tension pulling at her insides. He quickly poured a cup, then handed her the ceramic mug.

"Cream and sugar are on the table. Help yourself. I'll be back with the food in a sec."

She added cream and sugar to her mug and smiled as she took the first soothing sip. Masaki was in his caretaker mode, busy making certain she didn't have to lift a finger while he buzzed around the room plating their food.

"Mas, you know I can cook too. Why don't you let me help?"

He said nothing as he walked over to the table carrying both their plates. "I know you can cook," he answered. "But, you're recuperating."

She held up a finger. "No, I'm already recuperated. Now I need to get back to business at hand."

Masaki paused slightly before he walked around to the other side of the table and sat down to eat. "I know you're healed, Oshun. But, I need you to humor me. It's hard for me to shake that image of you helpless, almost lifeless on the ground."

She noted the worry etched into his face. It was as if the memory of her shooting alone brought him physical pain.

"Mas, I get it," she countered. "But, we didn't come up here for a leisurely vacation. We're here to regroup. We need to talk about this."

Masaki put down his fork and stood up, moving toward the island in the center of the kitchen. She wasn't surprised by his pacing back and forth. Whenever Masaki was angry, or contemplating something significant, he moved. The fact that she'd catalogued that bit of information away was another reminder that she was more attached to Masaki than wisdom allowed.

"You lied to me for months, Oshun. You moved into my home knowing who I was."

She turned slightly toward him as she watched him fight for control of the anger simmering just beneath the surface.

"I didn't know who you were Mas until our meeting at the diner. I only became aware of a possible connection between you and the Yakuza when you showed up at the fire."

"But, you still moved in with me," he responded. His voice was peppered with a hint of betrayal as he locked gazes with her.

"I did a thorough background check and I couldn't connect you definitively to the group. I tried to end things, Mas. I tried to stay away, but you insisted."

She stood up, meeting him at the island, touching her hand to his. "I moved in because I wanted to prove you weren't my enemy. I wanted something that would let me keep you in my life. It was dangerous and foolish. But, I wasn't thinking about my position in the Council. I only cared about being able to be with you."

It was the truth. The moment she realized Masaki had some sort of connection to her rivals, she should've walked away. The cut should've been clean and precise. Instead, her decisions had left them both messy and vulnerable to attack.

He pulled her into arms, weaving his fingers through her locs as he pressed a kiss to her temple. "You weren't the only one who made poor decisions, Oshun. I knew my desire for you would put you in danger. I lied to myself thinking I could protect you. But, deep down I knew someone would try to use you to get to me."

She understood the need he felt. It was infectious. It made you go against every natural instinct you had just to get a taste of what you wanted.

"Okay," she spoke softly, her voice cautiously leading them out of this emotional muck they'd found themselves stuck in. "Whoever's behind this was able to use our secrets to hurt us."

He nodded his head as a solemnness descended on his face. "Let's say we don't give them any more ammunition? Instead of stockpiling secrets, let's try this sharing thing I hear couples are supposed to do."

A couple? They'd been intertwined for nearly five months now. They'd done couple-like things, but never had she given herself the luxury of thinking of them as a unit.

The warmth of the idea filled her with a hope she wasn't certain was warranted in their current situation. With so much chaos in their lives, how could they even dare to hope for anything right now?

One glance at him answered that question for her. She might not know where things were headed, but wherever the events led, she knew she wanted Masaki by her side.

She smiled briefly as she nodded in agreement. "No more secrets, Mas. We do it together from here on out."

The matching smile he offered made a tingling sensation spiral down her spine, and spread out to all her nerve endings. Realizing she shouldn't let herself be distracted by Masaki's charm, she gave herself a mental shake and got back to business.

"If we're entertaining the idea that Izzy and Aesop either had help, or were put up to attempting to kill us, there must be something this anonymous person stands to gain. Have you come any closer to figuring out who would want to take you out of the game on your side? Who stands to win if you die, Masaki?"

She wrapped her arms around him when she posed that question, squeezing him to her as she let the words fall from her lips. The thought of what could've happened if Izzy and Aesop had succeeded made embracing him so much more than a desire. She needed the tangible reminder that Masaki was here, alive, and in her arms.

He pulled out of her embrace and walked them back to the table. While she sat down, he pulled his place setting across the table and sat in the chair next to hers. Apparently, she wasn't the only one using proximity as a stress reliever.

"Your people snuck us into this sleepy little town in the Pocono Mountains six weeks ago," he answered. "While taking care of you, I haven't thought of anything else but who could be behind this. No one under my command would dare something like this unless a big boss gave the okay. None of my contemporaries from other families would have that kind of power. This order had to have come from the top."

She raised a brow, not sure of where the glazed look in his dark eyes was taking him. "You have someone in mind?"

"Yes," he nodded slowly. "If I'm the high man on the totem pole here in this area, and someone in the organization is trying to kill me, that order had to come for the head of all families. The leader of the Yakuza in Japan, the Oyabun, has dominion over our tribes worldwide. If I'm marked for death, he's the only one who could've slapped his stamp of approval on it."

She watched him drift to that far-off place in his head again. Whatever he was pulling out of the recesses of his mind had to be significant, because he stood up again, pacing back and forth as his mind wandered.

"So, you think this head of all families—."

"The Oyabun," he interrupted.

"The Oyabun," she repeated. "You think the Oyabun put a hit out on you? Do you know why?"

He stopped pacing, locking his gaze with hers. "If he is after me, I have no idea why. Is it possible? Yeah. But if I'd fucked up enough to end up on the Oyabun's bad side, I'd know it."

He snaked a hand around his neck as he turned his head from side to side, stretching the muscles there before he continued. "Maybe we're thinking of this the wrong way. Maybe it's not about my enemy or your enemy. Maybe it's about our enemy. We're not the only organizations in the area. Between East New York, Crown Heights, Bed-Stuy, and Howard Beach, there are plenty of syndicates who would benefit from Brownsville and Canarsie going to war."

Oshun turned Masaki's suggestion over in her head. She had no proof of it, but everything he'd surmised seemed wholly possible. She didn't know if it was because her head would rather conjure up some outside force versus believing someone in her very own Council would try to kill her. Or, if it just seemed more practical that they shared a common enemy. Either way, she and Masaki were still faced with the task of answering these unknowns.

"If you're right, Mas," she continued. "This possible scenario makes our situation worse."

"How?"

"Because, if you're anything like me, you've got more enemies than you know what to do with."

10

Oshun trudged up the stairs after a day spent playing "Guess the Big Bad" with Masaki. For most people, she was sure the exchange would've ended after a few moments. But, when you were raised in the underworld, you inherited enemies like precious family heirlooms, their hatred cultivated and passed down from one generation to the next.

Mentally exhausted, she showered, put on a crop top, a pair of comfy sweatpants, and wrapped a satin scarf around her locs. She turned down the linens, prepared to bury herself beneath them when restlessness began to unfurl in the pit of her stomach.

She took a breath and contemplated ignoring the signs. But, she knew if she laid down with feelings of anxiousness twisting inside her, she'd be up all night and miserable in the morning.

She walked back into the ensuite bathroom, grabbed a tub of coconut oil, hair clips, and a comb before heading down to the living room. Never one to waste an opportunity to be productive, if she couldn't spend the night sleeping, she may as well twist her hair up.

There used to be a time when any free time you had landed you in Masaki's bed.

She flinched at the reminder her traitorous memory insisted on shoving in her face. No matter what she felt for him, they weren't a typical couple dealing with standard matters of the heart. There was so much more to be considered than just doing what felt good. They each needed time to deal with everything that was happening to and around them.

Determined to let sleeping dogs lie, at least for the moment, she headed for the living room, parking herself cross-legged on the floor in front of the couch. A quick press of the remote and she was watching television as she began the long process of re-twisting her locs.

She'd just dipped her fingers into the coconut oil when she heard, "You want help?"

She looked up to find Masaki standing in the doorway. Topless, with a pair of sweatpants on, he was the epitome of desire. Carved muscles throughout his torso and a dick print that demanded her attention from across the room, all he needed was a flashing red light to complete the warning he should come with.

"I'm sure you've got better things to do," she argued. "Did you get a chance to talk to your mom yet tonight?" *That's right, throw his mother in his face to kill some of that sexy he has going on.*

He pushed off the door jamb and walked toward her. "Yes, I did. Even though I'm using a burner phone to call her, it's not wise to stay on too long. Your father and his people are treating her well, that's all I needed to know. So, there's nothing keeping me from helping you."

He moved closer to where she sat on the floor, looking

edible in those damn sweatpants. Either they were extra thin, or his fucking cock was so heavy it looked like a solid rod was hanging between his legs.

She closed her eyes to give herself a reprieve. Looking at him, with his cocky smile and easy nature, had her so damn thirsty for him, she wasn't certain she could control herself for much longer.

"I even took the time to call Seth Stein and see what's going on in my organization," he continued.

"What did he say?"

Masaki shrugged his shoulders. "He still doesn't know anything definitive about who could be after us. He's following some leads and will get back to me. He says that for now everything appears quiet on the home front. Suggested both our seconds might be the only two involved in this mess."

He took a deep breath, slapping his hands on his muscular thighs. "Either way, I've done all I can do for now."

She offered him a bit of side-eye, silently calling bullshit on his sudden desire to help her with her hair.

"Need I remind you," he added, forcing her to look up at him and rejoin the conversation. "We've been hidden in the mountains for six weeks. Helping you twist your hair is just what I need."

He sat behind her on the couch, then spread his legs to make room for her to lean back against it. She was about to protest his help again when she felt his fingers bury themselves in her hair and lightly massage her scalp.

She tilted her head slightly and smiled as she spoke, "You sure you remember how to do this? I don't need you destroying my locs."

He leaned down, placed a kiss on the side of her mouth and moved his mouth near her ear.

"I remember everything where you're concerned."

The low timbre of his voice tickled her ear and caressed the exposed curve of her neck. She settled between his legs, welcoming the playfulness between them. The last six weeks had taken them from easygoing lovers, to patient and care-taker. She was afraid the fiasco they were attempting to find their way through had swallowed up the fire that made them, Oshun and Masaki.

They quietly twisted each of the long locs on her head, keeping a quick and comfortable pattern. Every time his fingers grazed her scalp, a tingle of electricity passed through her making her ache for him.

When people talked about the erogenous zones of the body, very rarely did she hear of anyone talking about the scalp and hair. Getting one's hair done probably seemed mundane to most. However, to her, letting someone get close enough to play in her treasured strands denoted an intimacy she didn't share with most people. If you were granted permission to touch her hair, Oshun trusted you.

They worked in concert until they were finished, and her hair was de-frizzed, and neatly tamed. She gathered her locs on the top of her head, pinning them in a noble crown, then tied a headscarf around her head, protecting their meticulous work.

She stood up. Unprepared to assume this would be leading where it usually did, she attempted to step away from him when he caught her hand. He gently pulled, and she eagerly followed until she was straddled across his lap.

He shifted beneath her and she could feel the obvious swell of his cock through the thin material of his sweatpants. "You up for this, Oshun?"

She let her eyelids fall closed, leaned her head back, and swiveled her hips to allow her mound to graze across his length. Even with clothes on, the sensation was profound enough to have her hissing through clenched teeth.

"I'm fine," she answered quickly.

She continued to swivel, reveling in the blessed friction their clothes and movements were creating. She was almost lost in the lull of their rhythm when she felt his finger caress the scars from her bullet wound and resulting surgery.

"Oshun?" His reply was terse. He wasn't going to let her ignore his question. That was Masaki, always pushing her to face things she'd rather forget.

She ran a hand through his hair, and let her fingers travel down the side of his face, until they were tracing his lips.

"Please, Mas," she whispered before planting a deliberately light kiss on his mouth. "I don't want to be your patient tonight. I just want to be..."

He snaked his hands around the deep curve of her hips until they palmed her ass, kneading each cheek firmly.

"You just want to be what?"

She stared into the depth of his obsidian gaze and for the first time spoke the truth of what her soul felt. "Yours," she whispered as her voice shook with emotion. "I just want to be yours."

He felt the weight of her words against his heart. In all their time together, she'd blocked every attempt he'd made to claim her. After months of trying to break down her barriers, she was finally opening the gates of her heart to him.

"You've always been mine, watashi no joō." His queen, a nickname he'd given her because of the meaning of her name. But it was true. She'd always been his queen, his heart, his everything.

"Hold on," he whispered, and lifted them both from the

couch, heading directly for the stairs. When they reached the upper landing, he walked through the open door to his room.

He'd balked against them having separate rooms when they arrived at this house hidden away by the heavily wooded mountains. But, Oshun's doctor had insisted they needed every inch of space in her room to attend to her medical needs. After she'd shown signs of recovery, he'd waited for her to invite him back, but she never had.

He hated being away from her, but he understood discovering your lover was a sworn enemy was a great deal to process. Instead of bulldozing his way through like he normally would, he waited for her to tell him when it was time for them to be more than what necessity dictated.

He sat down on his bed, maintaining his hold on her and her position across his lap. Loving the pressure of her weight plastered against his clothed cock, he moaned in satisfaction. The truth was this moment made him love everything about her and the way her body responded to his nearness, his touch, and his need.

He pulled her crop top off, and delighted in the feel of her skin beneath his. Its rich warmth was like silk under his fingertips. Lost in the sensation of his skin against hers, he wasn't prepared for the shock of cold that spread through him when he felt her pull away. Slightly dazed, he looked down between them, and realized his fingers had grazed her raised surgical scars.

"Do they still hurt?"

"I'm not in pain, Mas."

He went to touch her there again and was met with the same response, a retreat she didn't seem to want to explain. It wasn't until her saw her wrap her arm around herself placing her closed fingers against them that he understood she didn't want him to see the scars. She was hiding them, or more importantly, hiding herself from him.

"In Japan, when a dish is broken, we don't focus on the fissures or the brokenness of it. Instead we fill it with a precious metal, making it useable again, and then celebrate the new creation. Without those fractures, the new creation wouldn't have been a possibility. You were perfect before. But, these scars that remain are living proof that you cheated death and won. They are proof that you are the strongest woman I know, and that your strength is the sexiest thing about you. Don't ever hide your strength from me, or anyone else."

He placed a firm hand on her back and pulled her to him, rolling their bodies until they rested on their sides facing one another. His kisses started at the center of her forehead, going down the bridge of her nose until his lips met hers in a soft peck. When he tried to move on, she threaded her fingers through his hair and deepened the kiss. She opened her mouth, inviting him into her warmth, moaning in satisfaction when he finally allowed his tongue to slip beyond her lips, to let her taste him as he did the same to her.

He pulled out of her embrace, and slid down the length of her, allowing his kisses to pepper her skin as he lowered himself slowly. He avoided her attempt to deter him from his decided path, holding her wrists tightly to her sides.

This was them, the constant push and pull for control. From the first time they'd laid eyes on one another, there was always this unspoken battle to see who would decide their fate. He'd always assumed it was her way of playing hard to get. Her way of always proving she was the one in charge. But, now he saw it for what it really was, strength, the innate ability to lead, to command.

And damn if his dick didn't stand at attention in salute of all that power.

When he reached his destination, he continued placing

the barely-there kisses on her mound, pulling away playfully when she lifted her hips, chasing his touch.

"Masaki, please," she begged as her body quivered beneath him.

"Shhh, baby. Let me help you."

He slid a single finger down her slit, taking only a second to ghost his digit over the tip of her clit before he continued to her opening. He licked his lips, dangerously close to letting his tongue take the place of his fingers, when he found her slick and ready for him.

Unable to resist sampling her flavor, he eased two fingers inside of her as he simultaneously caressed her clit with the tip of his tongue. The way she bucked her hips in response told him he'd made the right decision. Usually he would savor the moment, torture her for as long as both of them could stand it. Tonight was different. Tonight, he wanted her to have everything she wanted and needed. Tonight, he wanted her to understand that anything she asked for was hers for the taking. He needed her to know she had his heart, and that meant he'd die to see her receive everything she required.

He moved his fingers expertly, scissoring them as he caressed her soft flesh from the inside. He increased the in and out motion of his fingers as he planted his face between her slick folds and latched on to her clit, suckling, licking. From the animalistic sounds she filled the quiet air with, he was torturing her in the best way.

He kept up his rhythm, continued his assault until he could feel her muscles tightening around his fingers, and when he knew she was at the edge of release, he replaced his tongue with his thumb, and quickly climbed until his lips were at the perfect height to devour hers.

When their lips touched, when she opened to him, taking his tongue inside and allowing them to both share the heady flavor of her lust, she splintered beneath him. Burying her nails into his shoulders as she held on through the cresting waves of her release, she cried out in ecstasy. The biting sting of her nails nearly breaking his skin coupled with the friction from her moving so desperately against him, had his balls pulling up tight in his heavy sac. He removed his fingers from her cunt, quickly shoving his sweatpants down just far enough to allow his dick to spring free. The feel of his roughened hand against the tender, throbbing flesh made him bite his lip in a strange mix of pleasure and pain.

He stroked himself, racing head first into the orgasm that was just out of his reach. She pushed his hand out of the way and replaced it with hers. He closed his eyes, let his head hang back, and gave into the electric sparks clawing at him from the inside. With the gentle scrape of her nail across the domed cap of his cockhead, his climax crashed into him. Stealing his breath, seizing control of his limbs until the last jet of cum left his tip, landing across her bottom lip.

Without an ounce of shyness, she smiled at him and eagerly licked the errant strip of cum from her lip like it was the remnants of a sweet treat. The sheer sexiness of it made his limp cock twitch with a half-assed attempt at getting hard again.

He leaned down, kissing her, loving the taste of the two of them mixed together. This was how it was supposed to be. The two of them together, one indecipherable from the other.

He struggled to catch his breath for a few moments, then left her in bed as he headed for the bathroom. He cleaned himself quickly, then returned to her with a wet washcloth to attend to her.

When he was done, Masaki sat on the edge of the bed, grabbing her hand between his and kissing the back of it gently.

"We've never discussed cum play before. It wasn't my intention to..."

"We both know if I hadn't have enjoyed it, I wouldn't have engaged in it. No apologies."

"I know we exchanged test results when you moved in," he hedged. "But, I'm still clean. There was never anyone else once you and I became intimate."

"I never doubted your fidelity, Masaki."

"And now that you know who I am? Do you doubt me now?"

She shook her head as the high apples of her cheeks rose, gifting him with a wide grin.

"Now that I know who you are," she began. "Now that I know I don't have to protect you from my world, I think I'm more in love with you than I ever was."

Her words rendered him speechless. He'd known how she felt. The fact that she always came back to him no matter how difficult things became between then was more than enough for him to understand the depth of her feelings for him. He'd known. But knowing, and hearing her say the actual words for the first time...he could've sworn his heart seized in his chest for just a fraction of a millisecond in response.

He planted a quick kiss on her lips before hopping into the bed next to her, gathering her in his arms and letting the comfort of her warmth soothe him.

"It's good to know I'm not out here in these streets by myself." She chuckled against his chest, and he squeezed her tighter. "I love you too, Oshun," slipped from his lips just as he closed his eyes and fell asleep.

11

Oshun burrowed into the warmth enveloping her. She didn't need to be conscious to know she was exactly where she wanted to be, her body naked and intertwined with Masaki's.

It was amazing the difference a day made. Yesterday, and every day before that, she'd wondered if they could trek beyond their obvious issues and find a way to be together despite the difficulties they faced. This morning, she knew there was only one answer to that question.

Yes.

She loved Masaki. That wasn't a new development either. He'd owned her body and soul from the first. The only barrier to that was the life she led. She didn't want to risk her world infringing upon his. But now, there was something freeing about the truth. It exposed their secrets and weaknesses, giving them nothing left to hide.

The threat wasn't over, not by a long shot. But knowing she would face this threat with him comforted her deep in the essence of her being.

She was about to snuggle deeper into his embrace when

she heard the landline ring a single time and then fall silent again. She eased herself out of the bed, making certain not to disturb the sleeping man next to her.

She grabbed her sweatpants and crop top and waited until she'd dialed her father's burner, before quickly pulling her clothes on.

"What's wrong?"

The single ringing of the landline was their code. It was his way of alerting her to trouble. They'd worked out that system when she was a kid. If he ever needed her to be aware and ready to move, he dialed the landline wherever she was, and found a subsequent way to send her the actual message he intended her to have.

"Someone tried to hit us last night," her father stated. His voice rough and direct, he pulled no punches when delivering the information. Her father wasn't a man of many words, and that proved to be an attribute in their line of work. You always knew what Zion Sampson meant, because he spoke plainly.

"The Council?"

"No, the decoy house in Baldwin," he answered.

"Is Mrs. Yamaguchi all right?"

"Shaken up. When I got word of the hit, I moved her to another location quickly."

"This isn't good. Masaki is going to lose his shit over this," she responded. She rubbed her temple trying to stave off the headache she could feel building behind her eyes.

"No, it isn't good," he added. "And not just for the obvious reasons."

"What's that supposed to mean, Daddy?"

"Outside of you and Masaki, I only gave that information to one other person, Oshun, and we both know who that is. Unless he's laying bloody in a ditch after having that info forcibly pulled from him, someone showing up to hit that specific location could only mean one thing."

"We've found the person behind this," Oshun answered. She rubbed the back of her neck as tension tightened the muscles there. "There's also another problem, Daddy. This person is trying to flush him out," she continued. "His mother has no connection to his business. The only reason he'd want to hurt her is to bring Masaki out of hiding."

"Agreed," Zion answered. "What do you want to do about it?"

If their enemies had come for her one living parent, there would be no question how she'd handle things. She would strike back hard. But, this was Masaki's mother. Although she was certain of what his answer would be, Oshun couldn't make that decision for him.

"Are you going to tell him who we suspect is behind this, Oshun?"

Oshun gripped the phone tighter as a knot formed in her stomach. She'd promised Masaki no more secrets, but would full disclosure be the best plan of action here? Telling him about the attack was one thing. However, giving him a target, someone to blame for the threat against his mother, was another matter.

This wasn't some random soldier in Masaki's army that an attempt had been made on. This was his mother. Masaki had a temper that sometimes made him reckless. Oshun wasn't certain informing him of her findings would help or hurt the outcome of this fucked up situation.

"I don't think there's a need for detail right now," Oshun answered. "We'll keep this between you and me for now."

Decision made, she forced herself not to worry about the consequences, and moved on with the conversation. "Daddy, make certain you take care of yourself. Get off the streets. If this son of a bitch comes for you, I'm gonna wage war against motherfuckers in these streets, and it's gonna be bloody."

"You know Zion is the original gangster, love. These young ones out here ain't got nothing for me. You tell Masaki I'll keep his mother safe as promised. I'll contact you when we get settled in the next spot. Stay safe, baby girl. Keep your eyes open and your Glock ready."

"Always, Daddy. Always."

She ended the call, still staring at the phone in her hand. "Apparently shit is about to get real."

She returned to Masaki's room in time to see him turning over in his sleep, reaching out for her. She watched him search for her for a few moments more, wanting him to enjoy the peace brought by last night's pleasure and subsequent sleep.

All too soon, he lifted his head from the pillow, ink black strands standing in multiple directions at once, the look of a man who had earned the tranquility good sleep brought.

"Come back to bed," he murmured as he dropped his head back to the stack of pillows beneath him. She walked over to him slowly, sat next to him, and ran her fingers slowly through his hair. A glance from her was all it took for concern to bleed into his features, wiping away the contentment that had shone in his eyes only moments ago. "What's wrong?"

She watched quietly as he pulled up in the bed, resting his back against the headboard, and fixing his gaze on her again. "Oshun, what's wrong?"

"They're trying to flush you out, Masaki."

She could see him calculating the unspoken pieces of her message. She knew the exact moment he'd connected all the dots when he closed his eyes, took a slow breath, and quietly asked, "Did she survive?"

"Yes," Oshun answered, and watched as he released the

breath he was holding in a rush, sucking in gulps of air as a desperate mixture of fear, relief, and anger seemed to pour over him. "She's fine, Mas. Daddy took care of her. He called me as soon as it was safe."

"Where is she?"

She raised a hand to his face, her thumb gently stroking the side of his jaw, attempting to sooth the tense muscle ticking beneath it. He was angry, rightfully so. His body tensed with each breath, his muscles instinctively flexing, visibly preparing for the unseen battle.

"Masaki, listen to me," she said in a soothing voice. "They are trying to scare you into rushing back. But, we're smarter than that."

He nodded as she spoke, his body language slowly relaxing with her words. He focused on her face, allowing her gaze to pull him out of the steely rage bubbling just beneath the surface of his skin.

"Okay," he answered. "What's the plan?"

"We're going to use my crew to help us set a trap," she responded.

With a pinched brow and eyes narrowed into slits, his skepticism was obvious. He folded his arms over his chest and tilted his head slightly to the side.

"I thought we couldn't trust either of our crews right now, Oshun?"

"I'm not talking about the crew I run with now. When you're in this life, you've gotta have an old-school crew you can always run back to when all else fails. I have a few people I can trust that aren't attached to my Council. But I can promise you, you're not going to like it."

He shook his head and pursed his lips. His displeasure evident in the silent communication. "An attempt was made on my mother's life, Oshun. There's not much about the situation to like anyhow."

He was correct, this situation had already gone to shit when they were ambushed at the diner. The healing bullet wound in her side was proof that circumstances were getting worse by the minute.

They were in hiding. And now the enemy had disregarded the unspoken rule of leaving family out of the street war. Well, if the villain hiding in the wings could break the rules, so could she and Masaki.

"If our mystery pursuer wants to play dirty. I say we play dirtier." She smiled as she pulled her burner cell from her pocket, and dialed a number from memory.

The phone rang twice on the other end before the call connected and she heard a familiar female voice say, "Hello?"

"I need a favor," Oshun answered.

"It's been how many years since I've heard from you, and that's how you greet me?"

"I know," Oshun returned. "But the last time we linked up, you told me to lose your number if I was determined to walk my path."

"Well, apparently, you didn't listen to me," the familiar voice answered. "Because, you're still calling me, and the word on the streets is that you're still ridin' dirty. What do you want?"

Oshun smiled at Masaki as she spoke into the phone and answered, "A friend. I need a friend."

It was late when they crossed the GWB and entered New York, and even later when they made it back to East New York, Brooklyn. This area was hit or miss with Oshun. She technically was in enemy territory, but that seemed to be an occurrence happening often lately.

It didn't matter. She drove an unmarked car with tinted windows, making certain not to draw attention to herself in any way possible. Anonymity was the name of the game she was playing tonight.

She glanced over at a tense Masaki as they sat at a stoplight. He hadn't given her a genuine smile since he'd heard about his mother. She couldn't blame him. He needed to hone every thought he had right now and focus on how to get them out of this situation safely.

She turned onto Fountain Avenue and drove until she came to the intersecting Flatlands Avenue. A left turn, and by the time she was in the middle of the block, she saw her invited guest waiting in a dark sedan.

Oshun parked the car and killed the engine on the vehicle before she turned to Masaki. "You ready to do this?" Her question first seemed to fall on deaf ears, his stoic facade unmoving as she waited for his answer.

"I'm not happy about this, Oshun. But then you told me I wouldn't be when you first thought up this crazy scheme. I still think we should reconsider. There has to be another way."

Oshun patted his arm as she noticed the two passengers of the car parked in front of them get out, and walk toward Oshun and Masaki's vehicle.

The pair was comprised of a man and a woman. Both African American, each with a badge swinging from a metal chain around the neck. Both were obviously packing as they popped the button on their holsters, gun-hands resting on the butt of their weapons, ready to draw if necessary in the blink of an eye.

"All right, Oshun," the woman's rough voice spilled from her mouth in a growl. "I could be at home in bed with my fine-ass husband. You wanna tell me why I'm out here with you instead?"

Oshun nodded her head and answered, "I sure do." Oshun turned to Masaki briefly as she spoke. "Masaki, please meet my old friend Captain Heart Mackenzie Searlington and her Lieutenant, Bryan Smyth. They're going to help us end this mess."

Masaki sat in the passenger seat with his arms folded across his chest, and his finger tapping against his bicep. It was a nervous tell of his. Something he only did when his instincts put him on alert.

He was a criminal, was born into this way of life, and would more than likely die that way too. Trusting a cop, someone who was a decided enemy, didn't sit right with Masaki.

"Are you certain about this, Oshun? Fucking around with your cop friend, we could both end up in irons."

He could see the easy curve of her smile from the side of her face as she navigated through the dark Brooklyn streets. She was obviously comfortable with this situation, or either insane. The truth was, he wasn't exactly certain which at this point.

"Heart and I go way back. We grew up in the same church together. We still see each other on occasion during church functions. We chose different paths in life, but she's always there to help me when I'm on the right side of the law."

"You think she'll turn you in?" The captain didn't seem like someone to turn a blind eye because of friendship. The few minutes he'd been in her presence, she'd been brooding, focused, and intimidating.

"If Heart ever caught me doing anything illegal, she'd bust me in a heartbeat," Oshun answered. "That's not what this is about. She's not going to catch me, or you, doing anything. She's simply going to back us up."

Oshun took her hand off the wheel, and reached across the console until he felt her fingers stroking his thigh. He didn't know why, but whenever she took the time to touch him, it calmed him, eased the natural paranoia he carried like a second skin.

"Do you trust me, Mas?" It was a big ask, especially considering all they'd been through. And although he'd had a momentary lapse of judgement where she was concerned when he discovered her identity, deep down, he knew what the answer to that question would always be.

He pulled her hand from his thigh and raised it to his lips. He placed a gentle kiss there before lowering it to his thigh again and giving it a loving squeeze.

"With my life," he muttered. "I trust you with my life, Oshun."

She smiled again, locking her fingers with his as she continued driving. "Good," she answered. "Because the feeling is completely mutual."

"So, what's the first move? I know you've got some sort of plan," he stated. The one thing this entire fiasco showed him was that Oshun was capable and prepared. He'd been unnerved and scattered when she was shot. He had no idea what his next move was supposed to be beyond making certain she was okay. But even in her debilitation, she'd found a way to execute an escape plan all before she'd come fully out of sedation.

"Heart and her team," she answered. "They're the first part. We're going to lay low for a few days while she sets things up. When she's done, we'll move to the second phase of this plan, springing the trap. A few days, Mas, and this will be over. I promise."

Masaki nodded, and leaned back against the headrest. Nothing about this situation made him feel assured, especially with his mother's safety in question. But, his faith in Oshun eased the tightening around his heart, and gave him leave to breathe a little.

He smiled, as the first promising thought since they'd left their mountain hideout crossed his mind. He turned to her, watching her as she focused on the road in front of them.

"Finally," he breathed. "We get to kill them all."

Oshun's stomach churned as she thought about their next moves. Masaki was beside her, preparing for battle, and still unaware of who the villain in disguise was.

Keeping the truth from him weighed on her. There were only four people who knew the location of the hideout that was hit. Only Oshun and her father knew it was a decoy. Assuming Masaki didn't try to have his own mother killed, it meant she and her father had figured out who was behind their attempted murders.

For three days, while they were stowed away in a seedy hotel in Queens, hiding from their enemies until it was time to act, she'd held this knowledge. She could lie to herself and say it was because she didn't want to upset Masaki further. But, she knew that wasn't the reason.

When Masaki discovered the person chasing them, and for what reason, he would go on a bloody rampage. She held no compassion for the low life that had set these events in motion. She just didn't want Masaki to go off half-cocked and get sloppy, leaving blood on his hands.

If they did things her way, their devil in the dark would get what was coming to him. And, Masaki's hands would be clean when it happened. She texted Heart a single name after their clandestine meeting on Flatlands Avenue. A returned message this morning filled with a laundry list of details confirmed Oshun's suspicions. The person who'd organized her shooting was no longer a mystery. Well, not to her anyway.

Oshun stretched her shoulders, trying to release the tension they seemed to carry by repeatedly reminding herself of the plan. If everything went accordingly, and Masaki was safe, she'd deal with the fallout of her keeping secrets from him again later. Right now, her plan was to focus on getting things ready for tonight.

"What are you worried about?"

The sound of Masaki's voice invading her thoughts pulled her roaming mind back into the room. He was standing behind her by the time she was fully present, placing gentle but firm hands on her shoulders, rubbing the stiffness there away.

"I know what you're standing here worrying about," he whispered in her ear as he pulled her closer, surrounding her in his embrace.

"Really?" The one-word question, as well as the jovial tone she'd added to it were meant to deflect as well as garner information. She was certain Masaki had no clue what was going on in her head. But better to find out specifically what he meant, than spilling the beans earlier than they needed to be. "Well if you know so much, Masaki, why don't you share?"

"Nothing is going to happen to me tonight, Oshun. We've been over the details with Captain Searlington. By nightfall, we'll have the info we need to exact revenge against our enemies. What better protection for me to have than a police captain and her squadron of heavy hitters who are in my lady's back pocket?"

Oshun chuckled at the idea of Heart Searlington being in anyone's back pocket. That woman would pull through tonight for one reason alone, to keep her streets safe from a gang war she knew would erupt if Oshun and Masaki didn't get a handle on this situation.

"Heart will do her best to keep you safe," Oshun commented. "She barely tolerates me as a friend, but she certainly doesn't want me as an enemy. Fucking up where your safety is concerned is the quickest way to getting on my bad side these days."

She turned around in his arms, and pulled his mouth down to hers for a kiss. With the world about to explode around them, the simple gesture felt heavy and meaningful in ways that both shook and comforted Oshun. The delicious taste of him was slightly tainted by the fear permeating all her senses.

She felt the uncontrolled shiver pass through her body and hoped Masaki wouldn't notice it. But when he pulled her tighter to him, breaking the kiss, and wrapping himself around her, she knew very well he'd noticed.

"Hey," he whispered. The warmth of his breath caressed the side of her face as he spoke. "Nothing is going to happen to me. I'm coming back to you."

Oshun took a deep breath and stilled the chaos in her mind. She put on a soft smile, and stepped back to look at him. "You'd better," she commanded as she placed firm fingers in his hair, and pulled his mouth just above her own. "Because you and the captain will have hell to pay if you don't."

Masaki smiled, playfully pulling away from her and looking at his watch. "We've got a few hours before things get started. Maybe we should make the most of it."

"I'd like nothing more," she countered. She placed a hard and dirty kiss on his lips, taking her fill of him, demanding everything he had to give. When she was satisfied, she lifted the hem of his t-shirt and raised it until it was over his head, letting it drop to the floor when he was free of it.

Taking only a moment to admire the carved muscular beauty of his torso, she tackled his belt, undoing his buckle, and pulling it from the loops of his jeans as she did. A quick flick of her wrist and his jeans were undone. She unzipped them slowly, too afraid her eagerness might damage the very thing she was so desperate to get to.

She kneeled to the floor, letting her hand slide down his leg until it reached his workman's boot. With a knowing glance, he understood her intent, and lifted his foot so she could pull his boot and then sock off. After they'd completed the same process on the other foot, she moved back to his pants, hooking her fingers inside the band of his boxer-briefs, simultaneously removing his underwear and his jeans at the same time.

She watched the powerful muscles of his thighs tense as he lifted one leg and then the other to free himself of the pooled clothing at his feet. Her mouth watered at the site of him standing naked in the middle of that room. He was beautiful, strong, sexy, and most of all, hers.

She stood up, quickly removing her clothes. When she was naked, she extended her hand, allowing it to caress his already hard cock. Gently tugging on it with one hand, she used the other to point at the sofa a few feet away.

He willingly followed her, sitting down and eagerly spreading his legs in anticipation of what she had in store. She wasted no time taking him into her mouth. Tonight wasn't a time for slow seduction. There was a very real threat waiting in the darkness and they both knew tomorrow wasn't promised to either of them. If they couldn't be sure of tomorrow, Oshun would make certain they had tonight to satisfy their need for one another.

She slid her mouth and hand up and down his length, her clit throbbing every time the involuntary suckling sounds she made rumbled in her chest.

Masaki may have been on the receiving end of what was proving to be a glorious blow job in her estimation, but the work she was putting in had her juices flowing, running a streak of warm, clear fluid from her cunt down her inner thigh.

She heard his moans become deeper and louder above her head. She felt him tangle his fingers in her locs, tightening until it was almost too painful to move. He applied enough pressure to keep her head still, and began a rhythmic up and down motion of his hips.

"Fuck woman," he hissed through closed teeth. "You think you're slick. You think I'm gonna lose my nut after a few swipes of your talented tongue."

The pace and force he was using was punishing, but with each snap of his hips, she was that much closer to her own release. He hadn't touched her. But the way he was using her mouth, it felt dirty, decadent, and made every nerve ending she possessed spark with need.

"I was easy on you in the mountains," he hissed "But, here, I'm coming the way I always do." He continued as he leveled a few more strokes. "Buried deep inside my pussy."

He pulled free of her mouth, taking a few breaths to regain his strength, then he stood up and gathered his jeans that were on the floor, pulling a foil packet out of one of his pockets.

He laid the unopened condom on the side table and laid down against the length of the sofa, his head resting against the cushioned armrest.

He looked down to where she sat on the floor and curled his finger. "Come here and sit on my face."

God, the power in his voice made her quiver with need. She closed her eyes, a feeble attempt to prepare for the onslaught she knew was coming. Between the deep rumble of his voice and the sinister look in his half-closed eyes, she realized she was in trouble.

When Oshun opened her eyes, he was slowly stroking himself from root to tip, his finger slowly rubbing a circular pattern at the tip. When she licked her lips, he passed his thumb through the dew drop of desire at his slit and offered it to her.

She moved quickly on shaky hands and knees until she reached his side. She latched onto his offered finger with the desperation of a starving woman, moaning when his strong yet sweet flavor spread across her tongue. It was just a taste. A small taste at that, and it made her burn with a fresh wave of desire.

She stood up, bending one knee at the side of his head, and extending her other leg so that her foot was firmly on the floor. Her stance left her feeling exposed and needy as she straddled him. She was certain that was exactly the way Masaki wanted her now. He positioned himself directly under her, burying his face between her swollen labia, lapping at her clit, sending electric shocks of fire through her system with each pass of his tongue, each suckle of his lips.

"Mas, please," she cried. "I'm almost there."

He'd been eating her pussy for all of five-point-six seconds, and already the familiar tightening of her muscles just before she climaxed was now within her reach. Together less than six months and he knew her body well enough to make her drip with desire in moments.

It could be that practice made perfect. In fact, that's what she'd always believed; they'd sexed so much and so hard, he knew how to make her body sing with pleasure. But now, after all they'd been through, she understood that the pleasure he gave her had little to do with his remarkable sexual abilities, and more to do with his heart.

Masaki gave her everything when they made love. From the very first, he'd poured his soul into the only avenue she'd allotted him to express what he felt, what was in his heart.

The two fingers he inserted in her opening caused her walls to tighten again and become slicker, begging for more of the tantalizing friction they delivered. A few more strokes, and Oshun was bearing down on those fingers, riding the lightning bolt of electric need as she squirted the first wave of her release over his face. She tried to shield him from the next spurt she felt coming, but he grabbed her hand, cupped his tongue, and drank her desire like a thirsty man in a desert.

She collapsed in bliss, completely ruined by this man's ability to bend her body to his will. She felt him move from beneath her, until he was free from her legs and still-dripping cunt.

"Ass in the air, baby," he commanded. Oshun complied as much as her loopy brain would allow her. She assumed she'd followed his command satisfactorily when she felt him slide between her swollen nether lips and push until his sheathed cock was stretching her walls.

"That's right, take it," he hissed. "I want to be balls deep in my pussy when I blow this nut."

She was still sensitive from her first orgasm, but could already feel the next one clawing at her. His deep strokes were pouring more gasoline onto the simmering embers of her last climax. He changed the angle of his next stroke, his cap rubbing just the right spot, and she tipped over into oblivion as she came apart for him again.

"That's it, come on my cock. I want it all."

His request was almost comical. She couldn't have held back if she wanted, her body had ceased listening to her the moment he'd touched her. Whatever he wanted was his, and for the first time since this crazy ordeal began, she was completely fine with that.

As the last wave of her orgasm crested then ebbed, she felt his frantic need as he drove into her again. His hands planted on her shoulders to keep steady as his powerful, but uncoordinated strokes expertly battered her walls, bringing her to another debilitating climax. When her muscles seized in pleasure, he gave up the last vestiges of his control and spilled over into his bliss with a load roar.

He collapsed against her back, leaving delicate kisses where his fingers had held her in a bruising grip on her shoulders, and held her until his breathing slowed.

"If for no other reason than I could never willingly give this up, know I'll return," he whispered to her. "I love you, Oshun. No one is ever taking that, or you, away from me."

M asaki drove his car on the westbound Belt Parkway until he came to the Rockaway Boule- vard exit. The sun had just set on Canarsie, but with the bright streetlights New York was notorious for, he was more than visible to the knowing eyes that watched him drive down the street.

He spotted an unmarked police car following him, and knew it was show time. Before he crossed the next traffic light, he saw siren lights come to life in his rear-view mirror. A second later, Masaki heard the officer directing him over a loudspeaker to pull over, exit the car slowly, get on his knees, and clasp his hands behind his head.

He did as instructed. Three plain-clothes cops jumped out of the dark sedan, with bulletproof-vests on, their weapons drawn and pointed at him. He also noticed a crowd of people gathering, stopping to watch the scene unfold. He just hoped the right pair of eyes were watching him.

The police officers transported him back to the seventy-fourth precinct, and left him inside the same industrial inter-rogation room he'd been in when they questioned him about the shooting-deaths of Izzy and Aesop, and Oshun's near fatal injury.

Goosebumps caused the hair on his arms to stand at attention. This was all for show, but it still fucked with his instincts to be in the presence of the police, even when it was a planned sting.

A few moments after arriving, Lieutenant Smyth entered the room. He directed Masaki to stand up, and escorted him to another room down the hall. Masaki stepped inside of another industrial room with concrete walls and drab gray paint slathered across them. But this room at least had a few more furnishings than the lone table and four chairs of the interrogation room.

"Your office?" Masaki stood still as the lieutenant removed the handcuffs from his wrists.

"Yeah," Smyth responded. "We didn't want to chance anyone overhearing what we were saying in the interrogation room. I'm gonna get you wired, and test it out with my surveillance team. When we're good, we'll get things underway."

Masaki nodded even though his natural inclination was to balk at being an informant for the cops. You didn't snitch in his world. You handled your business and dealt with your enemies by the code of the streets.

He would've given anything to have things work out that way. But when these motherfuckers came first for Oshun, and then his mother, Masaki had to put aside his own code of street justice, and let the police handle this, at least for now.

Oshun was right. The moment he discovered his mother had become a target, his anger pushed through his defenses, and he was ready to go on a shooting spree. If Oshun hadn't been there to calm him down, and offer him an alternative to ferreting out their enemies and exacting revenge, the arrest scenario tonight would've been real.

Smyth took his seat behind the large desk sitting in the middle of the room and directed Masaki to take the seat in front of his desk. "Let me get your suit jacket before you sit down, and we'll begin," Smyth requested.

"My suit jacket?"

"Yeah, technology is a wonderful thing. Gone are the days of wires, and bulky cameras taped to the body. There's a high-powered audio-visual recording device in this lapel pin. My team can control the camera angles remotely as you encounter the suspect."

Masaki nodded, handed his jacket over, and was about to sit down when a familiar name on a Manila folder caught his attention. He pointed to the folder as he asked, "What's this about?"

The lieutenant stared at him strangely for a moment before answering Masaki. "You're joking, right?"

"Not particularly," Masaki responded. "We have immunity where this case is concerned. You double crossing us?"

"Be easy, Yamaguchi," Smyth cajoled. "We got this. Your C.I. papers are in order. As long as you tell the truth regarding these matters, we're not coming for you for crimes related to this case. This folder is completely focused on our target for tonight's operation. I put this together for you to go over, to make sure we have the details correct."

Smyth walked around his desk, sitting in front of Masaki as he spoke. "We've had the suspect under surveillance since you and Oshun gave us the intel. As soon as he heard you were back in town, he put out feelers for someone to do wet work. We were able to get one of our undercovers in."

"The target will pick you up, with our undercover officer, and they will take you to an abandoned warehouse near JFK.

We have plainclothes officers surrounding the perimeter. We won't let anything happen to you."

Masaki nodded his head, and took the folder the lieutenant offered him in his hand. He read each line carefully, recognizing most of the details as correct. However, the information listed for probable cause for suspicion of the crimes in question didn't make sense.

Decoy hideouts only known to Oshun and her father meaning only two people believed his mother had been present on those premises. Masaki could feel his blood heat from an annoyed simmer to a raging boil when all the pieces fell into place.

He kept reading until details began to create clearer pictures. He understood one thing now. He'd been deceived. By the woman he loved, and by the person he deemed his right hand.

"The picture in the back is of my undercover officer. At this point, I'd tell you to call your lawyer and have him look things over before you sign on the dotted line. But since Seth Stein is our target, you can either call another attorney, or I can get you a court-appointed lawyer if you like."

Masaki ground his teeth as he tried to calm down. He couldn't fuck tonight up. If this night when to shit, he'd be on the run forever. Any longer away from his organization, and chaos would ensue. No, tonight had to be the night they finished this.

"No, I've read it. I understand the terms," he uttered. "Give me a pen."

Masaki scribbled his signature in the designated places, the black gel ink flowing from the pen like blood. When he finished, he handed the lieutenant the folder, and leaned back, attempting to keep his calm facade in place.

"I need to call my lady before all this begins. Would you mind giving me the office for a few minutes?"

Smyth paused for a moment, staring at Masaki pointedly until Masaki put on a smile. "I know you guys have everything planned out," Masaki said. "But, I just want to let her know I love her, in the event I don't get the chance to say it later."

He saw something in the cop's eyes soften, perhaps he too understood what it was to face one's mortality. Smyth nodded and stepped out of the room, leaving Masaki there alone.

Masaki removed his burner phone and tapped Oshun's icon in his contacts list. He squeezed the arm of the chair he sat in, hoping to decompress the pressure he felt building in his skull with each unanswered ring.

"Hello," she answered quickly.

"When did you know?"

There was silence across the line. If he hadn't heard background noises, he would've checked to make certain their connection hadn't been lost. He took a deep breath. Yelling in this room would only draw unwanted attention to him, so he let his breath flow loudly in and out instead.

"I asked you a question, Oshun. When did you know my right hand, the man I trusted with my mother's life, was trying to kill us? When did you know? Was it when that motherfucker tried to end us both in that diner? Or was it when he tried to kill my fucking mother? When did you know? And when were you going to share that shit with me?"

O shun knew he would find out, had narrowed it down to almost the exact minute he would become aware of her deception. She thought she'd prepared herself for it. She'd known when she made the decision to keep this information from him that he'd feel betrayed. Who wouldn't? But she hadn't believed her reaction would be the quivering nerves that twisted her stomach.

She stole a glance at Heart Searlington sitting in the driver's seat of the unmarked surveillance van they were in. Heart keeping her eyes focused on the smartphone in front of her was about as much privacy as could be expected in their current close quarters. But privacy or not, Masaki wasn't about to let her out of this conversation.

"I figured out it was Stein when my father called me to tell me the decoy spot had been hit. If only you and he believed your mother was there, I knew he was the one that ordered the hit."

"And it never crossed your mind in the two minutes it took you to leave your room, and return to mine, that maybe I'd want to be aware of Stein's treachery? That maybe I'd want to end that son of a bitch before he had another chance at my mother, or the woman I loved, or me?"

"Masaki, listen to yourself," she pled. "You're calling me from where? A police station? You're talking about ending someone in a police station. This is why I didn't tell you, Mas. I didn't want to risk your anger getting in the way, possibly allowing Stein to go free. Or even worse, causing you to go off without thinking, without protecting yourself first."

"That wasn't your choice to make, Oshun." His voice was quiet, but she could feel the force of what he'd said reverberate through the line. "What gave you the right to make that decision without my input?"

"Because I love you," she countered. "I love you enough to save you from your own miserable self. And if you've got a problem with it, tough. We'll deal with that shit later. But right now, I need you to get your head right. Because so help me, Masaki, if you let your foolish anger fuck this sting up, or worse, you get hurt because of it, I will ring your neck my damn self."

He growled into the phone, the timbre of his voice low, and deep. "Don't think this shit is over because you say so. You promised me no secrets, Oshun. I won't forget this."

The line disconnected, and Oshun stared at the phone in her hand. She'd held her ground, made no bones about the decision she'd made. But the finality in Masaki's voice, the way he'd ended their argument, it rang eerily of a coming goodbye.

15

Oshun put her phone away and sat quietly in the passenger seat of the surveillance truck. She was fortunate the entryway to the back, where all the equipment and Heart's other officers were hidden, was closed. At least her shame was only visible to her quasi friend.

"I know it's been a long time since we've been involved in each other's lives, but you can talk to me if you need to," Heart offered.

It was tempting to unload everything that was sitting inside Oshun's chest right now. The pressure was so great, her breathing felt slightly labored as a result. What Oshun wouldn't give to confide her fears to another human being. When you were the boss, you didn't get to do that. Letting your guard down could be perceived as a weakness. Weaknesses were to be exploited in her world, and she couldn't leave herself open to that kind of threat.

"I appreciate it, Heart," Oshun answered carefully. "I just can't."

"Because I'm a cop," Heart replied with her signature smirk painted on her lips.

"Partly," Oshun responded. Being on opposites sides meant their friendship could only be taken so far. They'd known each other, would always be there for one another, but their ability to bond as friends was limited for one simple reason. Oshun embraced her truth. "But mostly because we both serve a purpose in this community, and I can't give up mine to follow yours."

Oshun held no shame in the life she lived, and the choices she'd made. For their friendship to flourish, Oshun would have to repent. She might run counter to what the dominant culture believed was honorable, but her path had saved an entire community. A community that even Heart with her best intentions as a police officer often forgot about.

"Fair enough," Heart replied. "But here's some advice to take with you. I almost fucked up the good thing my husband and I have because I made decisions for us without consulting him. Not once, but on several occasions. It took a lot of work for us to get back on steady ground. I may not support what you do, Oshun, but the way you and Yamaguchi look at each other, it's obvious what you have is worth protecting. Don't let this life you're leading cause you to lose your man."

Oshun pushed her head back into the headrest and glanced over at Heart with a smile. "Sounds like you've gotten smarter over the years, Searlington."

Heart nodded her head. "Of course, I have. It's why they pay me the big bucks as Captain."

A banging sound from the back captured their attention, breaking the levity between the two women. Heart turned around in her seat, and walked the small space that led to the back compartment of the vehicle. Oshun followed, taking a seat near the back doors where she had an unobstructed view of one of the many screens on the inner panels.

"So, once we brought Yamaguchi in, a call was placed to Stein, telling him his client had been picked up. We've been tracking his movements, he's at my precinct now," Heart stated. "The guy he's hired to take your man out is actually an officer of mine. We just need Masaki to get Stein to admit his role in the attempt on Mrs. Yamaguchi's life, as well as your shooting."

That was a lot to hope for. Especially since this was a supposedly impromptu meeting. How was Masaki expected to draw all of this out of him and not make the low life suspicious?

"Let's hope the lawyer feels chatty tonight," Oshun replied.

Heart waved her hand dismissively through the air. It was obviously an attempt at deflection to help Oshun feel reassured about Masaki's safety.

"He's a lawyer, Oshun. They're always feeling chatty."

Oshun appreciated Heart's attempt at diffusing her angst, but the truth was, she wouldn't be all right until Masaki was in her arms again. Even if the only thing he did was yell at her, she didn't care. She just wanted this ordeal over, and Masaki safe. Once he was safe, everything else would be fine.

Masaki slid into the back of Stein's car. It was an act that felt all too normal for the current situation. He'd known this man since he was a boy. He'd served as counsel to Masaki's father. Had been the only outsider allowed into his clan for as long as anyone could remember. How could he have been the betrayer?

"I know things seem difficult with this trumped up

charge the NYPD is throwing at you," Stein began in the reassuring tone he always used when he was attempting to comfort Masaki. "But, I promise their entire case is circum-stantial. The D.A. will never move forward with so little evidence. Everything about Izzy's death screams self-defense. They won't be able to make this murder charge stick."

Masaki narrowed his eyes and nodded his head. He was grateful that Stein believed his mood was a result of the fake murder charges levied against him. As long as Stein didn't recognize the seething anger and hatred Masaki harbored for his once advocate, the plan would work fine.

"I'm sure you'll handle everything Seth. You always do."

The elder man patted Masaki on the shoulder, and sat back against the cushions of the seat. Knowing everything this man had in store for him, the feel of his hand against Masaki's arm made him want to strangle Stein with his bare hands. But, he couldn't. Not if he wanted to walk away from all of this free and clear.

Needing a distraction, Masaki turned to his window and watched as the dark streets of Brooklyn rolled by. When he noticed they were headed west on the Belt Parkway instead of east, Masaki's senses screamed danger.

"I think your driver has missed the exit for Canarsie. We're nearing Bay Ridge now."

"We're not going to Canarsie. The cops have been watching us carefully since you left with Ms. Sampson six weeks ago. We've relocated to a more secure location."

Masaki watched as the Belt Parkway turned into the BQE, forcing himself to remain calm as they drove. He knew the police could hear and see his surroundings, but saying the wrong thing could tip Stein off that the cops were on to him.

Masaki continued to look out of his window as he moved his hand down to his knee and tapped out his anxiety. To most people, this movement seemed benign, an action someone absentmindedly engaged in when they were bored. For Masaki, it was really a way to direct the restless energy that arose when danger was near.

Danger. It had been a constant part of Masaki's life since his birth. But other than the fleeting moments that he thought he might lose Oshun to that bullet, he'd never felt more aware of danger's presence in his life than now.

He turned to glance at Stein one last time. As he committed every etched line of his betrayer's face to memory, Masaki's resolve bloomed inside of him.

This motherfucker will not be the end of me. He will not win.

16

"Something's wrong."

Oshun watched as all heads in the truck turned in her direction. Something was wrong, yet none of the officers watching the same screens that she was seemed to clue into that.

"Stein has changed the venue," Heart answered. "That's all. There's no need to panic, yet. We have a car tailing them, we won't lose Masaki."

"No," Oshun replied. "You see how Masaki keeps tapping his leg. He only does that tapping thing when something isn't right. It's like his sixth sense for when shit is about to go tits up. Something is not right. You need to pull him out of there now."

"We can't pull him yet. Nothing has happened. Just sit down and wait."

The captain's response made Oshun's anger swell. She didn't give a damn about this operation, only about Masaki. She wouldn't allow anyone to put him in danger, not even her friend.

"Heart, friend or no, if something happens to Masaki because you didn't listen to me, I will come for you."

She watched the stoic captain straighten in her seat, and level her heavy gaze at Oshun. "Friend or no, badge or no, if you threaten me, you'd better be certain you can back that shit up," Heart replied. The captain waited a beat, letting the tension bleed out of the moment before she continued. "I know you're worried, Oshun. I promise you, we won't let anything happen to him. Just let me do my job."

Oshun sat back in her chair. Her breathing was labored as she pulled her eyes away from Heart, and refocused on the monitors tracking the car, Stein, and Masaki. As far as she could tell, they were in Red Hook now. That knowledge didn't make her feel any better.

Red Hook was one of those communities that was very similar to Brownsville. Poverty had ravaged it. Somehow businesses with money began to see the value in the water-side area at the edge of Brooklyn, and decided there was money to be made there.

Now, old warehouses were turned into rental spaces for catering halls and galleries. But beneath all the prettiness gentrification brought in, the ugliness of the criminal world was still present.

"Captain Searlington, I've got Lieutenant Smyth on the line." Heart nodded her okay to the officer, and soon the call was placed on speaker for all of them to hear.

"We're still tailing the car. From the GPS tracker we have on the camera, we know they're somewhere near the water-front. When we get closer, we should have a solid location on the car," Smyth stated.

"Hurry up and get me a location, Smyth. I'll get you guys some backup from the local PD," Heart responded. "Be careful with this one, Bryan. Oshun says something's not right. If anything seems off, you pull Yamaguchi out immediately."

"Copy that," Smyth returned before signing off the line.

While Heart stopped to contact the local precinct, Oshun slipped quietly into the front of the truck, closed the connecting door behind her, and pulled her burner phone out. If Masaki was in trouble, she wanted all hands on deck. She couldn't leave it to the police to make certain nothing happened to him.

She thought of the most likely ally to answer her appeal for help in this area, and dialed frantically. She prayed she'd hear the telling, "Who dis?" on the other end soon.

"Emmons," she murmured. "Come on. Pick up, dammit. I need you to pick up."

There was no answer. Not even a voicemail to cry her desperate plea to. Oshun's chest ached with panic. The more she tried to think of allies that could and would help her, the less she was able to string a coherent thought together. She was the great organizer, and yet when it mattered, she couldn't come up with a basic plan to save her man.

Heart had called it. She'd counseled Oshun that she couldn't control everything. And now, when it mattered most, life had chosen this very dark moment to prove that point to her in a perilous way.

Masaki stepped inside of the dimly lit warehouse, calculating his next move. He was strapped, his gun sitting in the small of his back, if he needed it, another secured inconspicuously on his ankle. The cops had tried to stop him from bringing it with him, but an open-carry permit proved to be a valuable thing in situations like these. He'd have to thank Stein for that privilege when he put a bullet in him later.

"Not that big a fan of the new digs, Stein," Masaki commented. "But, I guess they'll do in a pinch. Anyone else attending the party?"

Stein stood there in his expensive suit, looking every part the mouthpiece he was. Masaki was pissed with himself that he hadn't figured the son of a bitch for the rat bastard that he was without Oshun's help.

There she was again, even when he was seething with anger, she was there in the middle of his thoughts, making everything better. By now, he should've accepted that as her role in his life. If he had, maybe the last set of words he'd spoken to her wouldn't have been in anger.

He rolled his shoulders, trying to release some of the stiffness there. It didn't matter how foolish he'd been, Masaki knew he had to make things right with her.

The heavy slide of the metal door opening pulled Masaki's attention away slightly. He watched a hulking figure step inside and slide the door closed again.

About time the undercover cop got here.

As the newcomer neared, the hair on the back of Masaki's neck stood up. Something was wrong.

The Caucasian man, an inch or two taller than Masaki, stood next to Stein. His bald head and broad chest just added to the menacing picture the stranger presented. From a distance, he looked similar to the undercover detective Lieutenant Smyth had shown Masaki a picture of earlier. But, upon closer inspection, the man's facial structure was more angular, where the detective's face was rounded. This was not the same man.

Although this threw an unexpected turn in Masaki's plan, it didn't deter Masaki from his goal. If this dude wanted trouble, he was just another body to dispose of when shit went down.

"Who's your guest, Stein?" Masaki's voice was calm, with no hint of the alarm he felt zipping through him. He casually moved toward a stack of boxes and leaned on them with his hands folded behind his back, and his ankles crossed. Keeping things calm was the only way to ensure he walked out of here alive.

"This is my new associate in a business venture I've recently taken on. His name is Mr. Charles," Stein replied. "Were you expecting someone else, Masaki? Perhaps the undercover detective you and Ms. Sampson had the police send my way? Fortunately, Mr. Charles recognized the detective from a previous encounter. Otherwise, who knows how this meeting might have turned out."

Masaki didn't react. He didn't allow anything but his objective of getting out of this scenario alive to determine his next move. He could see the expectation in Stein's eyes. The man was waiting for Masaki to tip his hand. "Not sure that I know what you're talking about, Stein. Not even sure I really care. Now, this new business venture, that seems like something I should be interested in," Masaki stated calmly. "Since you work for me, am I getting a cut?"

Stein laughed, and spared a knowing glance to his associate. One that screamed of some secret knowledge that only the two of them shared.

Masaki's lips bent into a smile too. He chuckled slowly, as he inched his hand around the butt of his weapon, securing it in his grip.

"Mr. Yamaguchi," Stein continued. "I'm afraid tonight will serve as my notice to rescind my appointment as your attorney. I've decided to take on bigger things, such as buying up the land you'd intended to lease from the Brownsville Council, and making a mint on a development deal from the city."

"Ah, so you plan to cheat me, Stein? That can't be right. You know how badly a move like that would be for your health. You might want to think about that again."

Stein shook his head. "I've thought about it in depth. The one-point-five billion I stand to make is more than enough to keep me healthy and happy, Masaki."

Masaki gripped the handle of his gun even tighter, readying himself for the moment he would have to draw his weapon. It was no longer an "if" situation. There was no way Masaki was walking out of here alive if he didn't set it on the man he once trusted. The cold, blank look of indifference in Stein's eyes told Masaki this had devolved into a situation where words wouldn't help.

"Even if I weren't going to kill you over this, Stein, which I most assuredly am, how do you think you're going to get away with this? The Brownsville Council is never going to sell to you."

"Ah, and you would know this since you're fucking their leader, right?"

A chill ran down Masaki's spine. Any delusion he had about Stein only wanting him dead was completely erased in that moment. Stein intended both Masaki and Oshun to fall prey to this deal he was making.

Masaki eased the gun out of its holster, knowing he had to be careful, but quick, if he was going to blaze his gun before Stein's henchman. As it was, Masaki could see the man carefully sliding his own weapon from behind his back.

"I actually approached both your right hands to see if there was a possibility of brokering a deal," Stein offered. "I mean, I knew you wouldn't go for it, but I needed to see if she would. I offered both Izzy and Aesop ten million dollars each to either convince the two of you to go along with the sale, or to take you and Ms. Sampson out of the game. Guess what? They each chose to off you and your consort. Imagine my surprise when I realized money could in fact buy loyalty."

"Too bad it can't buy you a longer life," Masaki countered as he raised his gun arm, aiming it at the muscle Stein had hired, taking the large man down with two bullets to the head. Suddenly, Masaki heard return fire. He ducked behind a barricade of boxes, peeking around them to see Stein walking toward his hiding space with a raised revolver.

"You weren't half the man your father was, Masaki. He would never have made the concessions you've made as leader of the Canarsie Yakuza."

"He also didn't make as much money as I did either," Masaki yelled as he continued to watch Stein move closer to his crouched down position. "The more you kill, the less likely people are to do business with you."

"It doesn't matter." Stein's voice was shaky with excitement. There was no doubt in Masaki's mind that sick fucker was taking some sort of pleasure in this. "When you're gone, I make this deal, and take over your leadership. It will all be mine."

Masaki waited a second more, until Stein was in perfect position, then pushed the boxes over until they collapsed on Stein. In doing so, Masaki lost his balance too, toppling over with the boxes as well. His gun slid across the floor as he attempted to break his fall.

Slightly stunned by the fall, Stein shook his head, and locked eyes on Masaki's spinning gun at the same time. They both lunged for it, scrambling on the floor on hands and knees, trying to wrap their fingers around it.

In the end, Stein's position placed him an inch closer to the gun, and he snatched it up a second before Masaki could get to it.

Masaki lay sprawled on the floor, half sitting, half lying down. He watched Stein carefully stand up as he kept the gun pointed at him. With a sinister smile and an overt air of confidence, Stein touched two fingers to his own brow in a mock salute to Masaki.

"'O Captain! My Captain! Our fearful trip is done, The ship has weather'd every rack, the prize we sought is won—'"

Masaki reached for his backup weapon attached to his ankle, aimed, and fired before Stein could recite another line from the famous Whitman poem. Simultaneously, Masaki heard the loud thunder of another gun fire, and waited for the impact, for the pain, and darkness of death to come. At such close range, there was no way he would survive.

He waited to see the bright light of the other side. Certain that this was the point an old film reel of his life should be slowly moving across his gaze. But at the moment, the only memory he could form in his mind was the very second he'd seen Oshun for the first time, and his need to make her his.

He heard more voices. Some familiar, but most not, as he continued to wait for the nothingness he believed death was supposed to bring. His gaze focused once more on Stein, refusing to give that bastard the satisfaction of seeing Masaki cower in fear. Stein wore a look of surprise on his face. His hand pressed to his chest, as a thick, spreading stream of blood slipped through his fingers.

A second later, Stein dropped to the floor. Masaki saw Lieutenant Smyth standing with his gun drawn, and smoke wafting in the air from the tip of its barrel.

After a quick glance down at himself, Masaki realized he hadn't been shot. Both Masaki's and the lieutenant's bullets had neutralized Stein before he'd had a chance to fire at Masaki.

"I told you, Yamaguchi," the smiling lieutenant said. "Be easy. We got this."

EPILOGUE

Oshun stood on the Canarsie Pier and smiled as the salty air tickled her skin. The moon, high in the sky, shone a calm trail of light across the water. The tranquil scene before her belied the near-catastrophic events of the night, soothing the excited energy that still burned through her.

They'd survived.

She'd heard the gunshots from the surveillance truck. She'd prayed Masaki wasn't the one dead when she heard Lieutenant Smyth report there were two dead bodies present. The fear that came with the wild scenarios clouding her mind nearly broke her as details were reported to them at an excruciatingly slow pace.

In all her years running the streets of Brownsville, fear had never consumed her like that. In hindsight, she knew it came from only one reason. She blamed herself for lying to Masaki, for messing with his focus before he stepped in front of Stein.

"I've always loved this spot," Masaki stated. "It's always

calmed me down when the world around me seemed to be losing its fucking mind."

She nodded, then turned around to face her lover. His arms were already open, waiting for her to step in. She quickly moved into the space and collapsed against the hard plane of his chest as soon as he wrapped her in his embrace,

"When I heard there were two men dead, I was so scared, Mas. I thought I'd killed you. I thought you'd died hating me."

Between the tears that slid down her cheeks, and the way she buried her face into his chest, Oshun's words were muffled into indistinguishable sobs. It was rare that anything moved her enough to bring forth tears. In her business, tears were weakness, and Oshun was never weak. But as she stood on the pier, wrapped in his arms, she understood that the only time she'd ever been weak was when she'd felt helpless in saving the man she loved. These tears weren't weakness, they were relief, a celebration of the gift of a second chance.

"Oshun, you saved me," Masaki answered in hushed tones as he lifted one of his hands to stroke her locs. "I kept hearing you yelling at me about being a hot head. It finally clicked when I was in that warehouse. I'm not happy that you kept Stein's involvement in this mess away from me. But now, I understand why you did."

He placed a lone finger under her chin, meeting her watery gaze with a smile. "This night has taught me that we've gotta do better at this trust thing," he stated as he wiped the tears from her face. "We've got to stop giving each other reasons to mistrust one another."

"What do you mean, Masaki? Giving up the lives we live, leaving behind the roles we play?" She shook her head. "We've both seen what would've happened if we weren't here. Aesop and Izzy would've sold our communities out to turn a buck. I don't want that for Brownsville, not after the sacrifices I've made to make it a place worth calling home."

He placed his hands on her shoulders, effectively bringing down her ire. The movement forced her to focus on him, instead of the problem she felt creeping up at her.

"Oshun, we are both where we need to be, where our people need us to be. But what we lack is openness between us. We're so used to living secret lives, and dealing with things on our own, we didn't know how to turn to each other when it counted." He slid his hands down her arms, wrapping his fingers around hers. "I want to know all of you. And I want you to know all of me. I don't want to continue bedding my enemy. Instead, I want to share my world with my greatest ally."

Hope bloomed inside of her.

"So, a truce? A union between our two families?" She smiled as the idea turned over in her mind. "That's your suggestion?"

He nodded.

"And what if our people, or our enemies, don't like that idea?"

He leaned down, joining his lips to hers. The demanding press of his flesh against her mouth made her ache. She moaned her satisfaction. Needing to taste more of him, she opened her mouth just slightly, allowing him to tangle his tongue with hers as they stood on the empty pier unbothered by the lack of privacy.

When he pulled his mouth away, they were both breathing heavy, both obviously affected by their passion for one another. He smiled, wiping his thumb across her bottom lip, watching aptly when her tongue snuck out between her lips, chasing the tip of his thumb involuntarily.

"If anyone has a problem with us, in bed or in business, there's only one solution."

She lifted a brow, her head tilted slightly as she waited anxiously for his response.

"We'll burn this motherfucker down together. We'll kill them all."

Oshun smiled, moving in closer to him, as she drew from their shared power. This was how it should have always been; them together, conquering their world, their organizations as one.

"You're absolutely right, baby," Oshun agreed. "If they have an issue with this alliance, they'll have sealed their own fate." She pressed a delicate kiss on his lips, and smiled again as electric excitement flowed through her. "We'll kill them all."

The End

ABOUT THE AUTHOR

 LaQuette is an erotic, multi-cultural romance author of M/F and M/M love stories. Her writing style brings intellect to the drama. She often crafts emotionally epic, fantastical tales that are deeply pigmented by reality's paintbrush. Her novels are filled with a unique mixture of savvy, sarcastic, brazen, and unapologetically sexy characters who are confident in their right to appear on the page.

This bestselling Erotic Romance Author is the 2016 Author of the Year Golden Apple Award Winner, 2016 Write Touch Award Winner for Best Contemporary Mid-length Novel, 2016 Swirl Awards 1st Place Winner in Romantic Suspense, and 2016 Aspen Gold Award Finalist in Erotic Romance. LaQuette—a native of Brooklyn, New York—spends her time catering to her three distinct personalities: Wife, Mother, and Educator.

Writing—her escape from everyday madness—has always been a friend and source of comfort. At the age of sixteen she read her first romance novel and realized the genre was missing something: people that looked and lived like her. As a result, her characters and settings are always designed to provide positive representations of people of color and various marginalized communities.

She loves hearing from readers and discussing the crazy characters that are running around in her head causing so much trouble. Contact her on:

Website: LaQuette.com
Email: LaQuette@LaQuette.com
Amazon: www.amazon.com/author/laquette
Facebook: www.facebook.com/LaQuetteTheAuthor
Twitter: twitter.com/LaQuetteWrites
Instagram: instagram.com/la_quette

OTHER TITLES

Wicked Wager: Texas vs. Brooklyn 1
Bedding The Enemy
Lies You Tell
Heart of the Matter: Queens of Kings: Book 1
Divided Heart: Queens of Kings: Book 2
Protected Heart: Queens of Kings Book 3
Power Privilege & Pleasure: Queens of Kings: Book 4
His True Strength: Queens of Kings: Book 5
My Beginning: Trinity Series: Book 1
Love's Changes

COMING SOON...

LOADED LONGSHOT

Texas vs. Brooklyn 2

Kandi Adkins, the executive manager of Sweet Sadie's Cosmetics, has her roots planted firmly in Brownsville, Brooklyn. Kandi knows what it's like to have nothing. Education and her friend's late mother, Sadie King, pulled her out of the mire of poverty and enabled her to grab hold to personal and professional security.

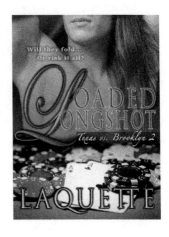

Life has taught Aaron Nakai to play his cards close to the vest. Reaching for more than you need only invites trouble into your life. That's what happened to his father, a man who died young attempting to make his mark on the world. He finds comfort and security living in his adoptive brother, Slade's, shadow. Aaron refuses to allow lofty dreams to rob him of the gains he made in life. Being Slade's lawyer and right-hand man suits him just fine.

When Slade needs Aaron to step out of the background and take care of an unexpected problem in New York, Aaron's quiet existence back in Texas is blown to bits by a quick-witted, sassy-mouthed fireball named Kandi. Their attraction is just as palpable as their distaste for one another, making the decision to wager their hearts and their careers a high-stakes game with potentially disastrous outcomes.

Will they fold? Or will they reach for a loaded longshot to win it all?

COMING SOON.

SEDUCTIVE STAKES

Texas vs. Brooklyn 3

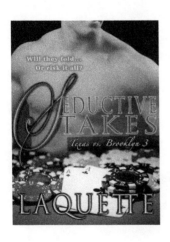

Azure Carlisle is simply tired. She's tired of always struggling to do the right thing only to have life slap her down time and time again. She climbed her way out of the projects of Brooklyn by getting an education. Her Ph.D. in Chemistry was her ticket out of the 'hood, but the lingering student loans from both her undergraduate and graduate degrees crush any dreams of personal advancement.

When the financial juggling game she plays every month begins to topple, Azure stumbles upon a way out. With an offer to clear her debts in hand, Azure is nearly burden free. The only thing she must do to escape financial ruin is simple:

betray the trust of the woman who offered her a job, and friendship.

Damien Mesías is the former CEO of Logan Industries. He's spent his life paying for the sin of his father's illegitimacy. When your dad is the result of a salacious affair between the respectably married tycoon and his maid, you're not as welcome to the family gatherings as your legitimate cousins.

Determined to prove his worth, and exact his revenge against the remaining Logan heir, his cousin, Slade Hamilton, Damien embarked on a dangerous path that nearly ruined him and the family business. Destroyed, divorced, and wallowing in a pit of despair, Damien aches for peace and forgiveness. But, with so much to atone for, those two things are elusive goals Damien isn't quite sure he can attain.

When an opportunity to get into Slade's good graces appears, Damien rushes to Brooklyn and finds his job is more complicated than he believed. One, the thief is a friend of the family, and two, she's the sexiest thing Damien has seen in a long time. Torn between his desire to do the right thing, and his need to have Azure, Damien is forced to make a decision that could destroy them all.

Will Damien ruin friendships, and Azure's life, by exposing her? Will Azure sell-out the people who have supported her to gain financial freedom? Or, will Damien's wild card play present seductive stakes that neither of them can walk away from?

NEWSLETTER

Hello,

 If you're interested in staying current with all the happenings with my writing, previews, and giveaways, sign up for my monthly newsletter at www.LaQuette.com.

Keep it sexy,
 LaQuette 💋

CPSIA information can be obtained
at www.ICGtesting.com
Printed in the USA
LVHW110536081118
596414LV00001B/22/P